A FOUNDATION IN WISDOM

STAGE ONE OF
AN ORTHOGONAL UNIVERSE

A FOUNDATION IN WISDOM

ROBERT LOYD WATSON

2012
MOUNT OLIVE, NORTH CAROLINA

Published in the United States by The Flying Wiener Dog Studio, LLC,
Mount Olive, North Carolina, USA

Version D8 R45 FP
Digital File Compilation Date: April 25, 2013

ISBN: 978-0-9889572-0-6

Disclaimer: All characters in this book are fictitious. I think that pretty much goes without saying. If you want to believe they're real, then, well, I'm not one to criticize your lifestyle. Just keep doing your thing, and don't sue me. Also, I'm not omniscient. That means any resemblance to real persons is entirely coincidental, and not because I'm a passive-aggressive jackass. Honest.

For Hazel, Tom, and Melissa

Christmas, 2012

STAGE I

Prologue

1. The Wind and Water's Ripples

The rain's splash on the road kicks up a fine mist. From a distance, it appears as a solid, translucent blur. Yet each individual bead of water spins and swirls in the sudden wind, unique and elegant. They shift and twist in harmony with their neighbors like the gears and mechanisms of a finely crafted pocketwatch twirl and tango.

A soulless leaf floats in a puddle on the side of the street, neither observing, nor observed by the mist above. The leaf dances - a celebration of life given by the wind and water's ripples. Its movements are graceful, not in the way of a well practiced dancer's, but like a marionette maneuvered by a skilled puppet-master.

The leaf starts to float down the street. It is now a quiet, but eager observer of the clockwork world. Its celebration continues into the intersection, its veins and curls highlighted by the red glow of the signal light above.

For a moment it waits, twisting and turning in pseudo-random arches. The mist around the signal light shifts to green. The leaf gently sways left and right, and is carried forward. Its dance is abruptly halted as it's crumpled, crushed, and torn into pieces by a speeding black, windowless van.

As the van approaches each intersection, the signal light shifts green, the highway helping push it into the horizon as quickly as possible.

"Please stay with me," the driver says.

"I have followed you all these years," the highway replies. "Why would I leave you now? After you have come so far?"

Thunder echoes in the distance. Specks of flickering light in the rearview mirror capture the driver's attention. The headlights of a following car, blurred by the intensifying rain, draw near. The two vehicles speed toward the forested outskirts of the city. The moon's light peers through breaks in the clouds, bathing the trees in silver.

The van approaches the entrance of the interstate. At its foot, a spot of sparkling gold mingles with the silver sky - the yellow glow of a malfunctioning signal light prompting the van to turn.

Lightning drowns the highway in blinding light.

"I must confess... I am a bit scared right now," the driver says.

"Understandable," the highway replies. "But you don't have far to go."

The van is joined by a third and fourth car. The three cars work hard to push the van off the road, while the highway struggles desperately to keep the van aligned. As the tangle fades into the horizon, thunder echoes across the hills. It screams as though the world were about to end.

2. The Scholar Extraordinaire

I am John Bartlebee, scholar extraordinaire.

What I love about a career in academia is that people pay me to think. Some people produce wheelbarrows. Some produce bricks. I produce thoughts. There are those who would argue that it's not quite the same... that there is a certain pleasure in producing something one can hold. That there is pride to be found in holding raw materials in one's hands, then transforming them into something useful, something beautiful.

To them, I say *pish-tosh*. To them, I say there is one simple point to be made. Anything which can be held can also be thrown. If *my* job was to produce wheelbarrows, and my wheelbarrows sucked, my customers would likely throw them back at me. Nobody can throw words. Nobody, except ventriloquists, that is. But anybody who parades about the block with a wooden man attached to their hand has no business telling *me* I've made odd choices on the path of life.

I travel the nation delivering lectures on the history of our great world. If you ask me, the current model of the university is flawed. I prefer the antiquated idea where I acquire a following and they pay me. Who wouldn't want someone giving you all their time, attention, and money? But no such models exist these days. If I want fanfare, I must travel myself.

It's still a fun job. For one, I don't have to produce anything that would hurt if it were thrown back at me. Second, if I "slip up" and tell a lie, I will be out of town by the next day.

There is no incentive to be correct *all* of the time, except maybe for ethics. When one has hordes of adoring fans, they hardly have time to read books. In the infancy of the twenty-first century, results matter more. I have mouths to feed... in particular, mine.

Recently, I've come to understand there are three sorts of people in this world. There are the practical, which live in the "real world." There are the imaginative, which live in their own world. Then there are the mathematicians, who may not be able to differentiate between reality and imagination, but sure know their Weyl Groups. The story I wish to share is my encounter with one of the latter.

That is when the storms began. I can't say the degree to which Sheridan... *Sheridan the Mathematician*... manipulated the weather, but he certainly did give the impression he could. The universe itself revolved around him in the way an anxious child hovers around its mother. But I didn't blame him for the rains which always fell this time of year. Late winter days in the Triangle region of North Carolina tend to be gray. The skies wept for the demise of winter, as Sheridan put it. I asked if it was sadness or joy. He told me it was just hormones - a natural part of growing up, and not to worry myself about it.

3. Smiling in the Freezing Rain

I met Sheridan on the side of the highway. From the get-go, he was an odd fellow. When I found him, he was smiling as he walked in the freezing rain. He seemed very at peace with the world.

I pulled over. He didn't notice as I crept up behind him, or when I flashed my lights. He only looked my way when I blasted the horn, and even then, he only raised his eyebrow slightly. The odd smile stayed glued to his face.

I asked him where he was going.

Sheridan paused for a moment, raised his other eyebrow, and grinned. "West," he replied. He stroked his chin as he thought deeply and carefully. After the long wait, he simply added, "Home."

By now, the wind had carried away all the heat from the car. Sheridan shivered and tried to hide it. I asked him if he wanted a lift.

"That sounds lovely," he said in a sort of sing-song voice. He looked back toward the city and stroked his chin again. "Where are you going?"

"I might be going to Oklahoma City," I said. It was practically a two-day, straight-shot down the interstate.

Sheridan grinned. "*Might*? You don't sound so confident."

"Well, I *am*."

Sheridan nodded. "Show your *Oklahoma confidence*. If

6

you're going to be wish-washy, you might as well stop at Memphis." He flashed a half-smile. I couldn't tell if he was laughing, sarcastic, or not quite right in the head.

I started to shiver. "Do you want to go or not?"

Sheridan stared at the dim lights of Raleigh one more time. "Oklahoma sounds fine," he said. "Just as long as it is not back the other way."

He didn't sound *Oklahoma confident*.

4. The Orthogonal Universe

Sheridan stared out the window, quietly whistling a tune. At first, I dismissed it. Then it entered my brain, wiggling around like a worm, chewing on my neuron receptors. It was a simple tune - consisting of five notes, the sequence different with each iteration. How long that could go on?

I had started to do the math in my head when I realized Sheridan had stopped whistling entirely. He was staring at me, wielding that odd smile of his.

Was he *trying* to get that tune stuck in my head? I couldn't quite read his smile - but I was certain he was amused by me. He nodded slightly.

I shook my head out of the daze. "Mint?" I held out an Altoid.

Sheridan smiled slightly. "Thank you. You would be surprised how many cars I've ridden in whose hosts did not have mints."

Hosts. I liked that. I wasn't just a driver. I was a host. And this wasn't just a car. It was an *an '88 Buick LeSabre* - the epitome of luxury and vinyl seating.

"I'd hate to think of myself as anything less than a perfect gentleman."

"Of course," Sheridan said. He nodded enthusiastically. "Having a car-mint to offer is simply polite."

"You don't want others to think low of you," I added.

"Of course not!" Sheridan said. "Manners are underrated

these days. It's common courtesy."

I nodded. "And it's not like you have to go very much out of your way."

"Exactly," Sheridan said. He tossed the mint into his mouth. "You don't have to go all out. Mentos suffice just as well as Altoids."

"Yes, but I'm a cultured man," I said.

Sheridan nodded. "I can tell... Classy."

For a moment, I believed the hitchhiker and I were gaining a sort of rapport. *For a moment.*

A fat fly struck the windshield with a loud *smack*. Sheridan stared at the goop, then asked, "So tell me, Bartlebee, what do you do?"

I pondered the precise way to word my business. I'd explained it many times before, but nobody seemed to quite get it. In the old days, it was common for professors, or *masters*, to travel the world taking on students. A student would follow his master. He would learn from him. Eventually, the students would become masters themselves, and acquire their own little followings. These days, people were concerned about things like "fellowships," "accreditation," and "post-graduation employment." I wasn't concerned with any of those things. My school was a school of the classical sort - operating out of my classic car.

"Call me a pioneer."

Sheridan stared briefly at a corner of the ceiling, where the fabric had begun to tear away from the frame. "A pioneer, I see."

"I travel the nation selling lectures."

"Selling lectures?" Sheridan chuckled, but looked a little confused. "As in books?"

"No. You see, I teach history." I reached behind my seat and pulled out a textbook. "History! It's not just for Thucydides anymore!"

Sheridan snickered. "With a slogan like that, I bet you sell quite a few history units!"

"I wish," I said. "After years of being declined positions, I founded my own school - a traveling school."

Sheridan grinned - his stupid grin somewhere between a laugh and an elated smile. "So you are a traveling professor? My, that is an unusual job."

I nodded. "It is. These days, it is. But it has its perks. It's *my* school. I am the president, chancellor, and provost -"

"*PCP*," Sheridan interrupted.

I smirked.

Sheridan smiled. "And just how does your school operate?"

I explained. "I deliver week-long seminars at a particular university before moving on. I teach classes no one else wants to, because it pays well."

"A noble motive, indeed!" Sheridan exclaimed. "Why, what better reason is there to act?"

Once again, he brandished the half-smile. It wasn't the weapon that bugged me the most, but how he used it. He'd sit with his hands neatly folded in his lap, perfectly still. He sat so still, in fact, that he seemed to disappear - except for the smile. He was like the Cheshire Cat. And, like any cat, he had the eyes of a creature just waiting for an opportunity to pounce. "Well, neither the faculty nor the students are really interested," I continued. "Most of the time, I throw in a few creative twists and few catch on."

Sheridan tilted his head. "Really? You can just make things up?"

I laughed. "It's amusing. Sometimes I get in trouble, but usually I can make an escape." Sheridan stared at me a moment before I repeated, "It's amusing."

Sheridan thought carefully, eyebrows curled. He had a peculiar way of thinking. I could almost see the gears churning in his head. First one eyebrow lifted, then the other. Finally, he spoke. "Perhaps in some parallel universe the twists are actually true and appreciated."

I shrugged. "Perhaps so. Perhaps you think me a bitter fool, and perhaps I am."

"Few artists are appreciated in their own time."

I couldn't help but notice Sheridan chose the word *artist*, as if I were practicing a craft. He nodded slightly, pleased with himself.

A dim light filled the sky as the moon shone through a thin portion of cloud. Pilot Mountain started to come into view. The mountain resembled a table, poking straight out of a relatively flat surface. Sheridan seemed quite fascinated by it.

"I'm on my way home from a disastrous seminar at Duke University," I said. "I don't think I would mind if we were on a collision course with a parallel universe. Maybe in the other universe things went better."

Sheridan shook his head. "A parallel universe would never intersect with our own. Every mathematician can figure that one out."

"I see. So you're a mathematician?" I asked.

Sheridan sat quiet while he watched Pilot Mountain come further into focus. He nodded his head vigorously. "Yes! And, as such..." He paused a second time and stroked his chin. "I know it is mathematically plausible that we are on a collision course with an *orthogonal* universe. In fact, it is highly likely."

"Highly likely?" I asked, eyebrows raised.

"Highly likely," Sheridan insisted. "Orthogonal universes are all around us."

"Is that normal?"

Sheridan nodded again. "Indeed."

"And what exactly *is* an orthogonal universe?"

"Think perpendicular," Sheridan explained. "Orthogonality is synonymous with perpendicularity."

I repeated under my breath, "*Perpendicularity*... Sounds... peculiar."

"Yes," Sheridan said. He smiled. "Call it *perpenpeculiarty*."

I lifted an eyebrow. "And how is this different from a parallel universe?"

Sheridan formed two parallel lines with his hands. "Well, it's geometry! Parallel planes will never cross. Likewise, a parallel universe would never intersect with our own."

He then made a "T" intersection with his hands and continued, "You get an *orthogonal* universe if you just take all we experience - the world events, the thoughts of man - and bend them."

"You bend them..." I slowly repeated.

Sheridan bent his hand into an angle. "Yes. Bend. The two universes differ until some great event, some time when they intersect. It's like two stories that converge to the same climax. After the intersection, they're the same."

The ideas tossed around inside my head like sweaters in a dryer. When they came out, they shocked me, and did not fit anymore. "I'd hate to be at the point where the orthogonal universe intersects with ours."

Sheridan nodded. "Yes, as would I. It would probably smart when it hits. And you would probably never even see it coming."

"I see."

I passed the time scanning the highway for anything that could resemble an *orthogonal universe*. Sheridan watched cars pass. He seemed unusually interested in our surroundings. I wondered if he was expecting an orthogonal universe to intersect the highway. I tried to picture what it would look like. Questions about the universe always made my head spin.

When I was little, my mother used to take me to the big church downtown every week. On our way back, we would always stop for gas at the Pump-N-Mart. The nice man at the counter would ask if we were heading home from church. Mother would nod. The nice man would then ask if I believed in God. I said I did, and he would smile and hand me a Tootsie Roll. This went on for a couple of years. Then one week, I asked the nice man where God came from. He kind of stared blankly for a moment, then said something along the lines of "well son... he created the world."

I said "I know, but where did *He* come from?"

The nice man froze. I thought he was mad. But now I think he just didn't understand the question. Mother told me not to ask the nice man any more questions. I never found out the answer. The question used to bug me, because it didn't seem to make sense for the world to be here.

Sheridan's statements bugged me the same way, and when I caught a glimpse of his eyes, reflecting off the passenger-side mirror, I saw he had the answer...

5. This Little Slab of Earthly Land

"Sheridan," I said. "Where exactly is *home* for you?"

Sheridan sat quiet for what felt like an eternity. I wondered if he just didn't want to tell me - or did not even know himself. I was about to speak when he finally said, "I am just following the highway. It will take me home."

I stared into the darkness. The headlights didn't seem to penetrate the abyss as much as they should. I knew the open land was outside, but it seemed like we were in a tunnel. That was when I noticed it.

For a moment, there was no sky.

There was clearly a storm when we left, which was not that long ago. In fact, I could still hear thunder. There were still occasional new droplets on the windshield. I *knew* the moon was full tonight. But when I looked up, the sky was completely, totally black.

As soon as Sheridan spoke, the clouds seemed to snap back into reality. "The highway said it would take me to the ones I loved." He paused for another moment. "And it would show me the world along the way."

I shifted in my seat and tried to view the sky through the side mirrors. "The highway said that, huh?" I asked. I still could not see the moon.

Sheridan's eyes lit up. "Oh yes!"

"I wasn't aware the highway could talk."

"Oh, it can." Sheridan nodded. "But so few listen."

"I see..." I muttered quietly. "Well... maybe in some *orthogonal universe* we all listen."

For the first time, Sheridan smiled genuinely.

* * * * *

I said, "I was thinking -"

"Because you are," Sheridan interrupted. He smiled.

"- that..." I stared at him. He nodded. "... you seem... awfully... *quiet* -"

"If you must know," Sheridan interrupted. He stared blankly out the windshield, leaving me hanging. Then he shook it off and smiled. "Mingo is waiting for me."

"Who?"

Sheridan continued to look out the window. "Mingo is my wife... my lady-love."

His reply made me pause. Originally, I had thought he was some random bum. To think he was married... it seemed too odd. "Well, I bet she'll be very happy to see you, then."

Sheridan smiled. "You have no idea."

I couldn't get past that smile. It looked forced. As he talked about her, his eyes lit up. Yet, he sounded a bit sad. And he was trying to hide that. Maybe they were having problems. Was that why he was way out here? That seemed unsatisfactory as an explanation.

The way Sheridan answered my questions was peculiar, but I couldn't place my finger on the reason why. He was staring at me, waiting for a reply. I forced one. "Then... how did you get out here?"

Sheridan went dead silent. Even his perpetual, stupid grin disappeared. I stole a few glances at him. He commanded more attention than the road, and I had to be careful. He finally muttered, "I don't want to say... You probably won't believe me."

"Why not?" I asked.

Sheridan was quick to answer. "You look like the sort of

person who wouldn't believe me."

I wasn't sure what to say to that, but somehow I got the feeling I should be insulted. He was probably right. Still, I was the *host*. I even gave him one of my best mints!

"Do you know who Scheherazade is?" I asked.

Sheridan nodded. "She was the queen who narrated *Arabian Nights*."

"She *had* to tell her stories," I said.

"Are you proposing to kill me if I don't tell you?" Sheridan asked. His perpetual smile returned.

"Well...." I drew out the syllable. "If I leave you on the side of the road, you might as well be dead."

I looked up at the sky. It still creeped me out. The clouds loomed above like a vast curtain. They were hiding something. I knew it. It felt like the entire universe above the clouds had disappeared - and all that was left was this little slab of Earthly land, slowly eroding away.

Sheridan was watching me stare. Perhaps if I left him in the *void* he really would be gone. That's when he said, "The world is about to end."

6. Promise You'll Believe Me

My heart hit the floor. At that moment, I knew I had picked up a looney.

I glanced at him. Whenever he was not speaking to me, he was usually watching the world. *Usually*. This time, he was watching me. He smiled. I lifted an eyebrow.

"What?" I asked, "Do I have something on my face?"

Sheridan shook his head. "You just seem quite fascinated by something out the window. What is it?"

I glanced out the windshield at the sky. As we headed toward Pilot Mountain, the road began to slope into the sky. The cloud ceiling was pretty close to the peak - perhaps only a dozen or two feet above.

"Nothing," I muttered. "It's... been a long day."

Sheridan nodded, slowly, as if he didn't believe me. "I see."

I nodded with him. He kept looking at me with big eyes - the sort of eyes a cat has when he sees a string. Before I could speak, he said, "The clouds won't eat *you*."

I gasped. "*What? How* did you know what I was thinking?"

"What else would you be looking at?"

He was right. Aside from the sky and the mountain, there was nothing out here. There were no buildings or even cars as far as I could see. Just a dim light in the distance - a gas station. I felt relieved, then puzzled. What was I worried about? I shook my head.

"You really need to stop freaking me out," I said.

Sheridan laughed.

"It's not funny! I'm trying to *drive*, remember?"

"Perhaps I should tell you a story to take your mind off the clouds."

"Perhaps..." I muttered.

"Perhaps!" Sheridan laughed. "Or we really shall perish!"

"Why did you tell me the world was about to end?"

Sheridan sat quiet for a bit. "Perhaps you weren't quite ready to learn that."

"Perhaps?" I asked.

"Perhaps."

"Will you stop saying perhaps!" I exclaimed. "You're driving me crazy!"

"Perchance," Sheridan said. He was the only one who found it funny. "I *should* tell you a story. *My* story. But you'll have to promise me one thing. You have to promise you'll believe me."

"I can't promise that!" I said. "That's not -"

Sheridan interrupted. "That's okay." He smiled again... the usual half-smile. "By the time I'm done, you will."

"Yeah..." I muttered. "*Perchance* we intersect with the *orthogonal universe*, too."

For the second time, Sheridan flashed a genuine smile. "We'll start at the beginning," he said. "The *very* beginning..."

I
The Non-Existence Proof

7. Some Things You Just Let Be

The light from a direction sign shone into the car as we passed under it, and I could see Sheridan was thinking hard.

"My story begins in Ebon, a small Roman village, about the start of the second century," Sheridan said. "Although one could say it really began much before then.

"It *truly* began with the creation of the universe. Everything in the world is the result of a long chain of events which stretch back to *the creation*. But the fact of the matter is, we have no proof the Earth *actually* exists."

"No... proof," I slowly repeated.

Sheridan nodded. "It's a conjecture - a mathematical conundrum. How do we prove the universe exists if nobody was around to witness its creation?"

"You got me."

"History doesn't record the whole chain. Hence, we don't truly know how anything enters this world."

Sheridan held his hands up, as if he were holding something long and thin.

"Such is the case with The *Giant Dachy*. Eight feet tall, with the face of a dachshund, the body of a dachshund, the butt of a dachshund, and was appropriately described as having 'generous proportions of length relative to width and height.' Nobody knows exactly how it came into being.

"What *is* known, is that some time in the early first century A.D., the elders of the Village of Ebon got together and decided the town had entered into a continuing spiral of moral decay. They decreed, *'all Good Young Men and Women shall be forbidden contact without the company of an escort.'* The Good Sons and Daughters complained.

"The council explained it was for their own good. After all, if Ebon was to be the region's shining apex of morality, it couldn't afford to have its young citizens heeding nature's call to mischief."

"Of course not!" I said.

Sheridan smiled. "It was about this time that the Giant Dachy took to chasing the Good Sons and Daughters into the fields, far from the village, running them scared for hours at a time.

"When the Good Daughters returned, the fathers demanded to know why they took off against the elders' wishes. The Good Daughters cried into their father's arms. Through streaming tears, they explained how the Giant Dachy chased them for hours, laughing menacingly without so much as a drop of mercy.

"The Good Sons were equally shaken. And so, all the fathers met with the council. Seeing how the village was under such a threat, the position of *Giant Dachy Lookout* was established.

"By the year A.D. 100, the original council was but a memory. The new council, the Good Sons and Daughters' children, were just beginning to grow old and feeble. Over the course of the many years, much had changed in the villagescape. However, one thing had not - the lookout tower."

- 1 -

During the day, the tower was clearly visible from all corners of the village. It stood against the blue sky, the town lay in its shadow. But at night the smooth surface and reflective stone made it glow slightly in the moonlight.

A young boy lay in bed and gazed at the sight. He thought about the eccentric lookout.

"Father?" the boy asked. He turned his head away from the window.

The father stood in the doorway. He tilted his head, then folded his arms over his chest and coughed. "Son! Sleep! Ranan is coming to town tomorrow. There will be great fanfare."

The boy exclaimed, "I want to be the tower-man!"

"The tower-man?!" The father laughed. He shook his head in disbelief. "*Why* would you want to be cooped up in a little tower all your life?"

"I want to go on adventures!" the boy exclaimed. His eyes lit up as he glanced at the tower and hills. "I want to fight monsters!" He flashed his teeth. "Rawr!"

The father laughed again. "Marcus doesn't fight monsters! He sits and alerts us if they come."

The boy stared at his father with big eyes. "But if they came, he'd fight them? Right?"

The father turned his head to the window and stared at the tower. He scratched his chin as he thought. "Well... they never come?"

"Are they scared?" the boy asked. "... of the tower?"

Nobody was scared of *Marcus*. He did not stand very tall. He was scrawny. He had short, black straight hair that showed his ears - the sorts of ears one would be more inclined to twiddle than to believe heard great beasts. And, of course, he spent all his time in the tower. He was mostly translucent. The villagers only thought of him when they noticed they were not being devoured by a Giant Dachy.

The boy stared out the window again. The father watched him for a moment, then smiled slightly and spoke softly, "Son,

the world is a complicated place. More so, the older you become. Some things, you just let be. Go to bed, son. Tomorrow
is a big, bright day."

8. Hope of Mathematical Purity

As I turned to glance at Sheridan, I saw he still wore the goofy grin he'd had since I met him. He let out a chuckle that was more like a snort - or a snort that was more like a chuckle. He looked at me and said, "Call it a *snuckle*."

I tilted my head and eyed him quizzically. He smiled. "What else would you be thinking about?"

I shook my head. "You... you did..."

He nodded. "Perhaps I've done you a great service... giving you something to ponder."

I stared blankly. He continued, "Since it does seem my tales are less than enthralling."

"Sorry," I mumbled.

"You know..." Sheridan said. "If Scheherazade told a bad tale, she would die. Maybe I should step it up, for fear you will abandon me on the roadside."

"The trick is to leave me wanting more each time we pass a rest stop," I said. "Or gas station... or wherever I could leave you."

Sheridan nodded. He waited until the next mile marker passed. "That gives me about fifty-three minutes."

"Until what?" I asked.

Sheridan smiled. "The trick is to leave you wanting more each time I'm about to complete a thought."

I smirked. "But, what if I don't want to know the rest of your thought? You need to work on building suspense.

That's what good storytellers do."

"Fair," Sheridan said.

He paused for a moment to think. The view of Pilot Mountain began to scroll off to the side of the car. He watched it carefully, as if he drew inspiration from it. Once it disappeared behind a tree, he resumed his usual position with his hands neatly folded in his lap.

"Mathematics intrigued Marcus from a very young age. He had befriended an aged Mathematician, one of the best performers of his day.

"Mathematicians at the time had the public eating out of the palms of their hands. Master Sophus and other number theorists appeared all over the empire, doing their acts in local eateries, bath-houses, and even before gladiator shows.

"By Marcus's time, number theory had lost the spotlight to applied physics. The people no longer cared about divisibility, primality, or even complex numbers. They wanted wooden blocks, springs, and pulleys. Master Sophus would shake his head. 'Nothing but prop comics!' Most of his fellow number theorists left mathematics and became bank tellers or executioners. Master Sophus never fell out of love with mathematics. He passed that love on to Marcus.

"Marcus dreamed of one day presenting his research at the conference in Rome. He dreamed of becoming famous. He dreamed of everyone knowing his name, but not knowing any himself."

I snickered.

Sheridan smiled. "Does that not sound like anyone I know?"

"Who, me?"

"I see noone else here."

"I don't necessarily want fame," I said. "I just want hordes of adoring fans."

Sheridan grinned. "Mathematicians don't need fame. They

only require two things to be productive - time, which Marcus had plenty of, and sleep. One would think sleep to be the bane of mathematicians - as one cannot devise proofs while sleeping. But Master Sophus knew of a magical bean that granted *the waking power of two men* when ground, soaked in water, and drank."

I looked down at my empty cup holder. "Coffee... *it's fuel for imagination.*"

Sheridan nodded. "Master Sophus knew well - perhaps even more so than anyone else in the village, save Marcus - the merits of a good foundation in logic..."

- 2 -

One gray, drizzly day, Marcus stood by the window, looking down at the village, watching the children at play. He thought carefully, turned to Master Sophus, and said, "I don't think the scientific method works too well for Mathematics."

Master Sophus scratched his chin, then tilted his head. "Did you deduce that from the window?"

Marcus nodded. "I deduced it from the children *outside* the window."

Master Sophus stood on the other side of the room, by a circular table. One leg was missing. The table was propped up against the wall and held his collection of scrolls and papers. They were carefully arranged so that they wouldn't roll off. It took him more time to remove a scroll than to read it. He glanced toward the window for just a second, mostly to humor Marcus.

Marcus continued, "Two young children look like they're planning to retaliate against a bully. It's an *experiment* in human nature."

Master Sophus nodded, without looking up.

Marcus leaned out the window for a moment, then popped his head back in. "Hypothesis... a stick to the head will only serve to stir the hornet's nest."

Master Sophus jumped. One by one, his scrolls began to roll off the table. He sighed as they formed a little pile by his feet, and renewed his interest in Marcus's observation.

Marcus continued, "An experiment that will, likely, need to be repeated. They have no proof their retaliation will always succeed. And I should know. I've seen this story play out a few times. There's no mathematical certainty."

"I believe it," Master Sophus said. "When an experiment succeeds, it only provides evidence a theory is correct. That's the idea, anyway... to support a claim by repeatedly failing to disprove it."

Marcus continued, "But a mathematical theory requires absolute proof. Logical proof. Concrete, definitive proof. Not a series of failing attempts to disprove it. There's a difference."

Master Sophus nodded in agreement. "So... why do you bring this up?"

Marcus turned toward the window. "I was thinking," he said.

"Man has a habit of doing that from time to time."

"Mind you, this is all in the spirit of good Mathematics," Marcus said. "I was thinking... pondering, really... how to be sure the tower is really here."

"Are you afraid it's not?"

"A good mathematician accepts only proof," Marcus said. "And by standing here, I've only *failed* to show the tower does *not* exist."

"But what about the floors and walls? Are they really here?"

"But the same question applies to those as well," Marcus said. "And the very Earth itself. Why, I do not believe I have any proof at all that I shouldn't fall into some great void."

"That would be a pity." Master Sophus stared at the floor and tapped it with his foot.

Marcus nodded. "Falling into a void would be a terrible fate - especially if nature were to call. It is terribly rude not to make use of the proper facilities for these things. I'd hate to desecrate the fabric of the universe because I've had a bit too much bread and wine."

"It's a conundrum," Master Sophus said. "For now you have *me* worried... and mind you, I am an old man. An old man doesn't need such worries."

"I do apologize," Marcus said. He hung his head a bit. "But inquiring minds need to know."

"It is you I will blame then," Master Sophus said, "When I cannot sleep, for now I know I've lived my entire life not having verified I am truly here."

- 3 -

That night, Marcus lay awake in bed. Clouds drifted over the moon, slowly dimming the light. Marcus watched the shadows fade, then disappear. He could hear Master Sophus's footsteps echo around him.

"Master, what are you doing up?" Marcus asked.

"I'm not up."

"You're not?" Marcus climbed out of bed. He felt the air rush around him as the bed flew into the sky. "Master!"

"Down here!"

Marcus could make out the faint outline of Master Sophus a few feet below him. The walls, furniture, and even the floor itself had disappeared. Surrounded by nothing, they were falling into the void.

"Are we really falling?" Marcus asked.

Master Sophus scratched his head. "It *feels* as so. But if nothing exists, could we not say we are rising, instead?"

Marcus could not tell what sensation he felt. "What would prevent us from coming out of the abyss, a -"

Master Sophus cut him off. "Don't say it! Don't say *anything*! This is all your fault, you know."

"I'm sorry," Marcus said. He hung his head. Or lifted it, depending on which way was up. "I did not mean to make the world disappear! I merely stated we could not verify its existence."

"Merely!" Master Sophus shook his head. "Merely is an understatement."

Marcus looked around. "Or overstatement."

Master Sophus glared at Marcus.

They drifted into a lonely sector of nothing. In the center sat a man of medium build. He had gray hair and a very elaborate magenta robe laced with gold and silver. He sat in deep thought. On his desk, he had two piles of letters - one pile of consonants, and another pile of vowels. Every so often, he would pick up two of the letters, try to combine them, then mumble something to himself and shake his head.

Master Sophus was the first to speak. "You! Good sir!"

The man slowly lifted his head and glared.

Marcus stared at the desk. "Who *are* you?" he asked.

The man said, in a deep voice, "I am the one they call... Fred."

"Fred," Marcus said.

"Fred," the man said.

"And what are you working on?" Marcus asked.

Fred shook his head and sighed. "I *was* working on a new word."

"A new word?" Marcus said.

Fred nodded. "I introduce new words into language."

"Ah!" Marcus exclaimed. "I always wondered where new words came from."

"Then tell me something," Master Sophus said. "Why... *Why* in the world would you choose to end a word with an ending like *-ght*!"

Fred cracked a sly grin.

Marcus's eyes lit up. "Wait!" he exclaimed. He nodded toward Master Sophus. "The world is gone because we could not mathematically verify its existence. Well, gone, except for Fred. Only the English language could exist outside any hope of mathematical purity."

"So we have not proven the language exists," Master Sophus said. He glared at Marcus. "Now don't you render us unable to communicate! You've done enough already."

Marcus shook his head. "Oh no, no! But we can *hypothesize* it exists. Each word we speak is a failed attempt to prove we cannot speak at all. Each day we live is a failed attempt to prove we do not live at all."

With that, Marcus was willing to accept the world's existence on a *tentative* basis. He found himself encased in darkness once more. *Master Sophus will certainly be relieved to have the world back!* Marcus thought. He wondered where the master went. He wondered where *everything* went.

Just when he began to worry the world may have disappeared after all, he slammed into the floor.

- 4 -

Marcus slowly opened his eyes. He lay on the floor facing upward. The sun shone directly into his face for a moment, then Master Sophus stepped in its path. "Was I asleep?" Marcus asked. "Was it all a dream?"

Master Sophus looked puzzled.

Marcus said, "I seemed to have lost track of my own existence."

Master Sophus smiled. "You'll make a fine mathematician one day."

Marcus climbed to his feet and leaned on the windowsill. He turned his attention to the village, stroking his chin as he thought. "Perhaps existence begins with purpose," he said. "Why am I here?"

Master Sophus shook his head. He snickered. "Fate has chosen you to be the watchman for the Giant Dachy."

Marcus smirked. "To think of what things I could be... if I were set free."

"You are free," Master Sophus said. "You could be anything you wished to be. You are the master of your fate."

Marcus smiled and nodded. "I'd like to think I could. But... no. I am a citizen. With duties. I think the village would simply have me be a number."

Master Sophus argued, "Then, you could be any number you wished to be!"

Marcus laughed. "Yes. Well, there are certainly a lot of numbers in the world."

"It's a big field," Master Sophus said. "What would you be?"

"Oh! To have the freedom to just say *a number*."

"Nobody is stopping you."

"Perhaps... seven." Marcus paused to think over his carefully selected choice. "Yes. I think I might like to be seven."

"Why seven?" Master Sophus asked. "For you did not pick nine or eighty. Surely there must be something about seven."

"There *is* something about seven," Marcus said. He looked out the window. "*Seven* would not be sitting here, manning a lonely tower in the middle of nowhere."

Master Sophus chuckled. "Then, why not be seven? Be seven and set free."

"Well... who *would* man the tower if I left?" Marcus asked. He shook his head. "No. I am not quite free. I need room. And board. Perhaps I am servant to these things. A number does not have use for them. Seven can be free to pursue all the wisdom in the world. And that is why I'm here... to get back to the purpose of my existence. To watch for the Dachy."

Master Sophus silently twirled the hairs of his beard around his finger. He then lifted an eyebrow. "So there's the problem. If the Giant Dachy does not exist, then you do not exist."

"I'd hate to not exist."

"As would I," Master Sophus agreed. "Otherwise, who would I be talking to?"

Marcus said, "But if the Giant Dachy does exist... and my duty is to watch for it, then I am tied."

"Perhaps you should not tie your own existence to the Dachy," Master Sophus said. He smiled. "Of course, a good mathematician wouldn't accept the existence of the Giant Dachy without proof."

Marcus nodded. "Perhaps... can we show the Giant Dachy exists? The existence of the tower implies the existence of the Giant Dachy. So we must prove the tower exists."

"No. I disagree," Master Sophus said. "The existence of the Dachy implies the existence of the tower! So we must prove the Dachy exists!"

"If we exist, the tower must exist."

"But then does the Giant Dachy exist?"

"This is absurd," Marcus exclaimed. "We are going in circles!"

"Indeed," Master Sophus said. "It seems to be that the entire world's existence boils down to our own. And our own existence boils down to the existence of the world. Perhaps we must prove the world exists."

Marcus looked down at the village once more. By now, the children had left and the adults were scurrying about, readying for Ranan's arrival. Marcus said, "They should thank us soon. For we shall prove they exist - and I do believe that is one thing man often takes for granted."

9. Then Marcus is Benevolent

Sheridan had a habit of pausing frequently. He seemed to be struggling to recall particular facts - stroking his chin and staring off into the sky. He'd crack a smile and I'd imagine he was about to say something amusing. But he'd go immediately back to staring at the sky. I'd clear my throat, tap the steering wheel, anything to grab his attention. He'd snap back into reality - and I'd realize he probably wasn't recalling anything at all.

He looked my way and grinned.

"You're peculiar," I said.

Sheridan nodded. "Perhaps. But I must inquire what lead you to that conclusion? However correct it may be."

"How can you question existence?"

Sheridan lifted an ear. "Oh? It's easy! You simply ask."

I shook my head. "No, no. How can you question *if* we exist?"

Sheridan stared at the car ceiling and hummed. "What do you mean?"

"It's a scientific fact that we exist."

"Ah!" Sheridan grinned. "Is it really?"

"Well, I'm here, aren't I?"

Sheridan nodded. "You know... some people claim that a statement is only a *scientific* statement if it is falsifiable."

"That doesn't make sense! If all scientific statements were false, wouldn't that mean..."

"No, no," Sheridan said. "Not *false*. I said *falsifiable*. It means, if I want to make a scientific statement, it should be possible to show it is false... or rather, put to a test."

I muttered. "Oh..."

"So it should be possible to prove we *don't* exist."

"But... *How*?! Wouldn't proving that, well..." I paused. "I don't know!"

Sheridan laughed. "Let's call it a *proposition*. We exist."

"Okay," I said. "What next?"

"Well... we have a couple days, at least, until we get to Oklahoma," Sheridan said. He grinned. "Now, let's put it to the test!"

"Hmmm.. Okay," I said. "How?"

Sheridan smiled widely. "We distinguish between the good and bad ways to go about the problem," he said. "So to start, I'll tell you more about Marcus and Master Sophus... Marcus and the master had been good friends for many years."

Sheridan stroked his chin again and cracked a grin. "*Many* years, indeed! But Master Sophus was growing very old and ill. Marcus didn't talk about it, but he knew Master Sophus's final days were upon him. Master Sophus often asked for time to rest. During this time, Marcus would cool off in the village fountain.

"On hot days, nobody paid much attention, as this was a reasonable thing to do. On cooler days, however, he would receive stares from those who discovered him. *Discovered*, because he made his best effort to hide behind the falling water-beads. If he were caught, he would usually say he was washing himself. The truth, though, was that he liked to people-watch, but not people-interact. There was a good reason for this. A good number of the villagers disliked Marcus. Or, rather, they disliked paying his salary.

"It wasn't personal, of course. Typically, nobody likes paying the police tax until they are mugged, or the fireman's tax until they are burned. However, those people tend to survive to happily pay their taxes. All the people who didn't mind paying the watchman's tax had been eaten by the Dachy.

"On this particular day, the village was in a rush. Ranan, the regional governor, was coming and hopefully bearing funds from Rome. Whenever he came to the village there was always a big festival. Half the villagers believed the village should be carefully tidied up, so as to put a good face forward. The other half pandered to Ranan's pity. If they looked like they needed aid, they would surely get it. Therefore, the resulting festival consisted of a potluck lunch with good intentions, but bad food.

"Marcus took no part in any of it..."

- 5 -

Marcus's attention was caught by the falling water-beads. Their twinkle in the sun captivated him, as they blinked in a seemingly non-sensical way: dim, bright, bright, bright, very bright, dim.

He would also watch, with great amusement, how they intertwined. He wondered if anyone else ever paid such close attention to the phenomenon. *Nobody I know has ever talked to me about such things as this*, Marcus thought. He said to the beads, "Perhaps it is our little secret."

"Hey, you! Marcus!" a villager called. "With you in the fountain. what will become of us should the Dachy attack?"

Marcus stared at the villager. He disliked confrontation. While he disliked his *duties*, he didn't mind his *job* too much due to the abundance of free time it afforded him.

"Yes! You should go watch the tower," a surly old man cried. "We're paying you, after all!"

Marcus stared at the two men and cleared his throat. He was about to speak when another voice, that of a rather large man with a mousy face, piped up. It was Ranan. "This is silly! Is this what you do with my aid?"

The villagers turned his way. Ranan exclaimed, "What are you paying for?"

"Protection from the Giant Dachy!" the old man replied.

"How do we know the Giant Dachy exists?" Ranan asked.

Marcus's conversation with Master Sophus on existence was fresh in his mind. He looked toward Ranan and smiled slightly. "Man is too wise to build a useless tower!" he exclaimed. "There is no reason to have the tower if the Giant Dachy does not exist. So there must be a Giant Dachy."

The other villagers looked at each other and nodded in agreement. "We are very wise," they said.

Marcus chuckled to himself. He fully expected the villagers to wander off and leave him be. But Ranan insisted on arguing. He stood with his hands on his hips, his stomach stretching as far out as it was wide. "But how do you know it is the Giant Dachy that the tower protects you from?"

"We never see any Giant Dachy!" another villager answered. "So the tower must work!"

Marcus hid a grin behind the water-beads.

"And Marcus's job hasn't been terminated!" the village crier argued. "So clearly his presence in the tower must be worthwhile."

"Right!" Marcus said. "My position *is* worthwhile."

"But your position is worthwhile only if you prevent us from being devoured by Giant Dachy," Ranan said.

"Well, Marcus knows the tower is there to prevent Giant Dachy attacks," the village crier said. "He just showed that because the tower exists the Giant Dachy exists... so that can only mean one thing..."

"He killed a Giant Dachy!" a villager exclaimed.

Marcus froze for a moment. He looked around in confusion as the villagers began to cheer. "He's a hero!" they exclaimed. "How did you do it?!"

Marcus scratched his head. "Actually... I've never seen a Giant Dachy."

The villagers stared at each other. "He must have proven to the Dachy itself that it didn't exist!" another villager shouted.

"Right," a second villager said. "But the Dachy clearly existed before, else we would be very silly for having built the tower. And we are wise."

"Clearly. Because if it existed now, then Marcus would be dead. And hence, so would we!" the other villagers cried.

Marcus's memory began to cloud. He scratched his head. He'd never seen a Giant Dachy nor remembered such an encounter. He thought, *If I did prove the Dachy did not exist, would that then wipe it from my memory?*

The crowd was cheering and applauding. Marcus liked the admiration.

"Let's just hope Marcus doesn't prove we don't exist!" the town crier exclaimed.

By now, the entire confrontation had grown quite large, as many passerby stopped to listen to the commotion. A wandering trader stopped with his wares. He stared at the town crier and tilted his head. He caught Marcus's eye and the two stared at each other like cats do. He had wavy blond hair and amber eyes that seemed to blend in with the ground. The sun caught the trader's hair, burning the image into Marcus's mind.

"Marcus is benevolent for having sided with us!" a man exclaimed.

Marcus watched the trader whisper something to Ranan. Ranan shook his head, brushed him aside, and laughed. "Hail Marcus!" he proclaimed.

"Hail Marcus!" the villagers echoed in unison.

Before Marcus could fully grasp what had happened, the

villagers swarmed the fountain and carried him off, cheering and applauding their hero.

10. An Information Hole

I didn't want to admit it to him, but Sheridan *did* make me ponder. I spent the next several moments trading stares between the road and the sky, contemplating the existence of both. I feared the road itself would vanish, and we'd fall into the abyss. The clouds - the infamous clouds loomed above. I feared the world above them had vanished.

I said, "It seems to me that Marcus does not have a good *grisp* on reality."

Sheridan smiled one of those odd smiles that I'd come to loathe. He shook his head, still grinning, and replied, "Arguably not much better than your *grisp* of the English language."

I stared at him. "What?"

Sheridan laughed. "It's *grasp*, my friend! One does not *grisp*, they *grasp*!"

"Okay! Okay!" I surrendered. "So I made up a stupid word."

"Stupid? Oh no-o-o-o!" Sheridan exclaimed. "It is a *lovely* word!" He nodded. "I would be proud to add it to my vernacular. Of course..."

"Of course? What?"

"Well, it is redundant," Sheridan said. "We don't need two words that mean the same thing. Perhaps a new definition for *grisp*... Let's see..."

I glared at Sheridan. His eyes lit up. "Ah! To *grasp* is to hold firmly. So let us say to *grisp* is to hold firmly, but not so firm that it is spelled correctly."

"What in the world does that mean?"

"It is like... one or two notches removed," Sheridan said. "It's a hold, but not as tightly as when one *grasps*."

I smirked and glared at him some more. "You're mocking me, aren't you?"

Sheridan shook his head. "Me? Of course not! But the car will not drive itself. Come on! *Grisp* the steering wheel! Ten and two!"

I shook my head. "Okay. Okay. Why don't you tell me more about Marcus?"

Sheridan smiled. "Marvelous idea. Marcus was quite shocked at the speed with which everything happened. While he was still trying to get a *grisp* on things, rumors about his accomplishment began to spread."

I rolled my eyes when he said *grisp*. Sheridan ignored it. "A particularly amusing aspect of news is how it travels. Once, it was suggested information travels at nearly the speed of light. Considering the Theory of Relativity, perhaps we see why news is stretched and warped as it travels through space."

"But news isn't mass," I said.

"It depends on how you market it."

I stared blankly at Sheridan. He nodded and explained, "The primary method of communication in those days was word-of-mouth. Such a method *hardly* guarantees what is delivered to you is what actually happened. In turn, this introduces some general confusion and surprise into the topic as information changes hands. There is a degree to which one could either confuse or take advantage of this phenomenon - known as the 'oh, really?' factor..."

- 6 -

The village crier stood in the town square. He proclaimed, "Marcus defeated the Giant Dachy!"

A villager ran to the wagon-builder. "Marcus *proved the Giant Dachy away* into non-existence!"

The wagon-builder then claimed to his adversary, "Marcus could *prove you away* into non-existence!"

"Oh, really?" the farmer asked.

Once it became known that Marcus could "prove things away," details about the encounter began to emerge. Stories were passed from villager to villager, with each trying to top the others. Nobody quite knew exactly what happened. It was an *information hole*. And information holes are frequently filled with bullshit. It wasn't long before the wagon-builder fell into the hole and found himself waist-deep in manure.

The wagon-builder met the horse-breeder at the village market. The builder had just heard Marcus's story from the farmer, and was eager to tell anyone who crossed his path. The breeder was tending to his horse when the builder took him by the arm, yanked him aside, and told him all about Marcus's encounter.

"I mean, Marcus was *literally* frozen in his tracks!" the builder exclaimed.

"Wow!" The breeder contemplated this for a moment. "Who de-frosted him?"

The builder lifted an eyebrow and tilted his head. "De-frosted?"

The breeder nodded. "Did the Giant Dachy have frost-breath or something?"

The builder scratched his head. "Uh..."

The builder and the breeder stood in the market, mutually confused. The muffled sounds of transactions cut through the air between them. After a moment, the breeder added, "You said he was frozen. Literally."

"Oh!" the builder exclaimed. "I didn't mean *literally* literally."

"Figuratively."

"Yes," the builder replied. "He was *figuratively* frozen in his tracks!"

The two men stood silent, contemplating the nuances of proper speech. The breeder then said, "That doesn't quite sound right."

"No... no it doesn't," the builder said.

"Doesn't quite have the same..."

"Punch," the builder added.

"Yes," the breeder agreed. "Punch."

"I see what you mean," the builder said. "He was *literally in a figurative sense*, frozen in his tracks!"

The two men stood silent for another moment, both uneasy with the conversation. They occasionally stole glances at the surrounding shops. The builder said, "This is silly."

"Yes," the breeder said. "Silly. I mean, I know what you mean."

"And I know what *I* mean."

"Of course," the breeder replied. "I wouldn't think you'd have said something otherwise."

The builder smiled and nodded. He then noticed his friend at the other end of the market. He ran to tell him the news. "You wouldn't believe what I heard! Marcus was literally frozen in his tracks, when -"

"Wow," the friend interrupted. "I didn't know the Giant Dachy could breathe ice!"

- 7 -

By that evening, the entire village had heard the good news. The villagers cheered their hero for having saved them from

the Giant Dachy. Marcus was paraded through the streets to
the hall of the village council. There, he would be received
by the twelve village elders to share a dinner in his honor.

Though, at first, Marcus was quite confused as to how
this all came about, he convinced himself that maybe, just
maybe, he had simply forgotten his encounter. If the Giant
Dachy was proved not to exist, then there would be nothing
to remember.

The villagers set Marcus down at the entrance to the council hall. At least half of the town had gathered. Villagers in
the back rows jumped up to see over the others. People in
the front rows shouted praise and questions.

"How did you unfreeze yourself?" one villager shouted.

Marcus stared blankly at the villager, dumbstruck. Before
he could attempt an answer, the twelve elders circled him.

"We would all like to shake your hand and congratulate
you on your most heroic accomplishment," the council leader
said.

As the elders began to crowd around him, he made note
of the *probable* existence of the hall. With the exception of the
lookout tower, it was the tallest building in Ebon. It only had
two stories, but the first floor had abnormally high ceilings
and doorways. He suddenly felt like he had shrunk, and
perhaps was entering non-existence himself.

That is absurd, he thought. He quickly dismissed the no-
tion that existence was relative to size. *Certainly there are some
things that can't be seen, but do exist. And, most likely, some things
that can be seen, but don't exist.*

Marcus was quite content to have all this fanfare and admiration, but by now, he was also significantly hungry. Still,
he couldn't simply ignore his hosts. As he started around
the circle, shaking the council members' hands and receiving
their gratitude, he thought about his stomach. He pondered
that if he were to shake only every fifth hand as he moved

around the circle, he would still meet every member before coming back to the starting man. *But I should eat sooner as I am skipping every four men*, he thought. *Clearly this is the best solution.*

And so, Marcus moved around the ring of council members, shaking every fifth man's hand. They were quite intrigued at this peculiar behavior. "This is the mark of a man who knows what he is doing", the council leader whispered to the man next to him. "He is saving us time by skipping so many of us, yet doesn't insult any of us by not receiving our gratitude."

When Marcus shook the last hand, the council leader proclaimed, "Let us eat!"

Marcus had little time to speak during the meal. Most of the council members were talking of his conquest. How, exactly, did he prove to the Dachy that it didn't exist? How did he manage the opportunity to speak without being devoured? It all puzzled them. It puzzled Marcus, too.

Yet, as Marcus looked around the room, he grew accustomed to the admiration. *It is very rewarding to have ones' life's work appreciated*, he thought. *Perhaps I can leave. Perhaps I can be sent on a crusade to see the world. Perhaps I could rid it of the other Giant Dachy.*

The council leader asked, "Tell me, Sir, how you managed to prove to the Dachy he did not exist? I really must hear the details of this great accomplishment."

Marcus swallowed his bite of food and proclaimed, "I am adept at non-existence proofs."

One of the other council members nodded enthusiastically. "Yes, you have a truly remarkable sense for the non."

"Indeed. I am a master of the non-sense," Marcus boasted.

Marcus sat back and welcomed the praise and approval. *Sometimes the world doesn't make sense*, he thought. *But, that doesn't necessarily mean one shouldn't sit down to eat when dinner is offered.*

In the back of his head, a quiet voice still nagged. It asked him exactly how all this came about. *How does one gather knowledge of something's existence to begin with? How does one obtain the knowledge leading to the knowledge of something's existence?* He wondered how people learn, and what the nature of this world must be. *How does one put all these answers together?*

The voice tugged for a while, making itself quite a pest while Marcus ate. He thought the food would have tasted better if it had not been present. However, the pie was excellent.

11.   That, You Must Find

I wanted to stare at Sheridan. Stare long, deep, icily. The road was twisty and I couldn't look away, but I just *knew* he had that goofy grin. For the first time, and not the last, I wondered if Sheridan was having fun at my expense.

"As I mentioned," Sheridan said. "Master Sophus's health had been rapidly declining. Marcus returned to find him confined to bed. Yet, despite his tiredness, the master was quite eager to hear all about the great ordeal..."

- 8 -

Master Sophus laughed and exclaimed, "Congratulations!"

Marcus grinned. "It was nothing, really."

Master Sophus shook his head and laughed again. "Well, perhaps now the villagers will put this whole thing behind them and leave us alone."

Marcus lifted an eyebrow. "What do you mean?"

"Well... now they'll stop pestering us about watching for that Dachy..."

Marcus interrupted, "Well... I proved *it* no longer existed. But..."

Master Sophus tilted his head.

Marcus continued, "Just think... They said I was a hero! I could be a famous h-" he lost his concentration.

Master Sophus sighed and shook his head. "Marcus...
you are wise enough to know the importance of humility."

Marcus forced a slight smile.

Master Sophus said, "Fame is a beast that eats a heart and
spits out a face."

Marcus stared at the ground.

Master Sophus added, "There's more to life than simply
being *known* for something."

"I know that," Marcus said, "but -"

"You can't tell me that -"

"- this could be my ticket out of here..." Marcus finished,
ignoring Master Sophus's interruption.

With that, Master Sophus paused, silent. Marcus fidgeted
uncomfortably. After several moments, Master Sophus sat up
in his bed. "Marcus. What is wisdom?"

"Wisdom?" Marcus repeated. "It means... to have knowledge."

"To... *have* knowledge?"

"To have it all," Marcus said. "To know all things."

Master Sophus thought for a moment. "I think you should
learn what wisdom really is."

"I'm wrong?" Marcus asked. He stared at the window.

Master Sophus lifted an eyebrow.

Marcus continued, "I sense disapproval. Do you not think
I'll be famous?"

Master Sophus shook his head and coughed. "I have no
doubt that you *will*. Someday. Someday, your deeds will
be told for centuries to come." He smiled. "It is quite the
thought, Marcus, the great hero."

Marcus nodded. Master Sophus wiped the smile off his
face. "Marcus," he said. "I want you to attend the great
conference in Rome."

Marcus's eyes grew wide. "You mean... *the* conference?"

The empire's mathematicians met once a year for a festival in bashing each other's work. Known as The Conference, it was a three-day winner-take-all contest. Mathematicians from all over arrived, wielding their best research, the remains of the public's affection at stake.

Master Sophus nodded.

"Do you really think I'm ready?"

Master Sophus nodded again. "Quite," he said.

"Wow..." Marcus muttered quietly. "I don't even know what to present. Perhaps... my proof that the Giant Dachy -"

"No, no, no." Master Sophus shook his head. "I have something for you."

Marcus's pupils grew as big as a cat's. He exclaimed, "Oh! Do show!"

Master Sophus reached for a roll of paper and handed it to Marcus. He unrolled part of the paper and inspected it. "It's blank?" he asked.

Master Sophus said, "It will teach you the nature of wisdom."

"How?" Marcus asked. He turned the roll over in his hands. He examined each side, looking for a clue.

"I want you to write," Master Sophus said. "If you insist on being the great Dachy crusader - then tour the countryside. Extract all you can from the experience. I think, then, you'll know what to present at the conference."

"The Conference..." Marcus said quietly. "It seems all too much. Me? In The Conference?"

"It is time," Master Sophus said. "Every mathematician will, at some point, need to defend his research. For no research is so credible it will escape the wrath of the lord of the conference... *the Referee.*"

Marcus's eyes grew wide. Master Sophus nodded. "Yes, fame is possible. It is hard, but it is possible. The conference is the key. It is a great triumph to defeat one's peers on the gladiator's stage, to win over the Referee, to be heralded the victor of the conference. Only then will you be awarded the ultimate prize - credibility of your research."

"Indeed," Marcus said. "That is true."

"But you must get there. Doors do not open themselves," Master Sophus replied. "No more than paths expose themselves."

"How do I open the doors? How to find them to begin with?"

"That is the foundation of wisdom," Master Sophus said. "That, you must find."

These were the last words Master Sophus ever spoke. After their conversation, Marcus bid the master goodnight. The next morning, Master Sophus never woke up.

II
The Quest for a Quest

12. Just Follow the Road

I wanted to say I'd met Sheridan before. It seemed so improbable. Of all the people in the world - to meet someone so familiar on the side of the interstate... it just... all seemed so strange. Yet, after entering Greensboro, the feeling persisted. Perhaps it was the street-lights. In the city, they were placed by the highway, yielding my first real glimpse at Sheridan. He had black hair, grown out, with a slight, bluish tint. The tint struck me as odd. I figured it should reflect the color of the street-lights. He caught me studying him, and grinned.

He said, "You look familiar, too."

I had no idea how he kept reading my mind, but I didn't have time to think about it now. I slammed on the brakes. Ahead of me, the road had disappeared. A black fog encompassed the asphalt, rendering it completely, totally invisible.

Sheridan gazed at the abyss. Its nothingness reflected off his eyes. I scratched my head and said, "It's as if that part of the world was deleted."

Sheridan laughed. "That's what I get for dividing by zero."

"I don't see what's so funny," I said. "We could've fallen off the face of the Earth!"

"Oh, you worry too much." Sheridan shook his head. "It's only the unknown."

"Yes!" I exclaimed. "Unknown!"

"You're afraid of the unknown," Sheridan said. "You-"

"No!" I shouted. "I'm not. It's just... I..."

I looked to the right. I knew an alternate route... a route through the mountains. I glanced at the sky and sighed. "Nothing," I said. "Nevermind it all."

Sheridan nodded. "Marcus was about to set out on the road himself." He glanced toward the void. "Sometimes the road hides many secrets..."

- 9 -

The days following Master Sophus's passing crept. Marcus realized he would make no progress toward Master Sophus's advice stuck in the tower. Life was short. Too short, in fact, to waste it contemplating the non-existence of a defeated monster.

The elders were disappointed to learn of Marcus's decision to depart. They did hope, however, he would make the Village of Ebon's name heard - and for that, they gave him their blessing.

Marcus wasted no time leaving. He sold the few things he could not carry, and set out onto the long, winding highway. The village disappeared into the horizon and soon faded to memory.

As Marcus gazed at the trees around him, he felt free for the first time. He pondered this feeling, as he'd never believed his position in the tower to be all that restrictive. Yet, as he stood in the road alone, he realized just how much the tower had confined him. The world seemed strange and foreign. The leaves looked different. The clouds he could not place. Even the very water of the stream he passed by seemed different.

Marcus stopped for a moment to watch the moving water. His reflection shifted and warped in the ripples. His black hair stood out against the water. He pulled at it, and wondered what struck him as "off." In the water, his hair looked a very dark blue. The shade of the water matched his dark blue eyes, so it appeared as though the water were moving through his head.

Marcus pondered this effect and believed it to be the most peculiar thing he had ever seen. "What sort of water runs *through* a person? All my life, I believed that water runs *around*. Could I be *touch-translucent*?" He gave himself a few healthy jabs in the rib, just to make sure he was real and tangible. He winced, but poked himself again, as it was good science to repeatedly test one's own hypotheses. *Master Sophus would be proud.*

And so Marcus went along in this fashion, poking and prodding and wincing. He had not gone on for long before he noticed that he had nothing to show for his research save a rather large bruise, and he contemplated how scientific progress is seldom recognized with any greater fanfare than one's own suffering. Indeed, he had only his own self from which to receive praise, and he had spent so long cheering himself for being a good scientist that he paid no attention to the foggy mist that had formed over the roadway. With his view partially obscured, he could only hope he would not be devoured by a Giant Dachy.

- 10 -

Soon, the mist became so dense that it prohibited a passable view of the road. As he walked, Marcus contemplated the crunching of the leaves under his feet. They were hardly visible through the mist, but curiously loud. The crunch almost echoed in a rhythmic pattern. He wondered what the road might be saying.

"*Marcus!*" Someone whispered. "*Mar-cus...*"

Marcus passed it off as only his imagination. But when he heard the voice again, he became fairly certain it was real. He replied, "Who are you? Show yourself!"

"*Mar...cus...*" the voice whispered.

"I am fairly certain you are not me," Marcus said. "For I am me! And as any good Mathematician will tell you, I can have but one identity."

"But, *Marcus,*" the voice whispered, "how is it you are certain my own name is not Marcus?"

"Is it?"

"No."

Marcus folded his arms in front of his chest. He glared around him - not knowing exactly where to fire his annoyed gaze. This only agitated him further, and he demanded, "Well... *who* are you?"

"Marcus! Down here," the voice called.

Marcus looked around the road for a ditch, cliff, or some dip in the ground. He saw nowhere anyone could be hiding. "Clearly no one is present!"

"Some things are right under your nose," the voice replied. "Look again?"

Marcus looked down at the road. "I see only the road and my feet, and I hardly am willing to believe my own toes would have many words for me. Last time I checked, toes were not the sort of beings which made pleasant conversation."

"I would imagine," the voice said. "For I have heard no such tales of anyone inviting their own feet to dinner."

"But who are you, then?" Marcus asked. "If you are not my feet?"

"Look below your feet."

"Are... you... the... highway?" Marcus asked. He slowly formed each word.

"Indeed," the highway replied. "It is very nice to meet you."

"It is... uh..." Marcus said. "Nice to meet you?"

"You sound hesitant," the highway replied. "Are you sure it is nice to meet me?"

"I find it rather odd the highway has many words for me," Marcus said. "It seems silly."

"Perhaps I find it silly a person-type has many words for *me*," the highway said. "But I am well-mannered enough to know that when others speak, it is polite to listen."

"Oh! I did not mean to offend you," Marcus said. "But you must admit... I don't know! But I will listen!"

"You are kind. It is not too much to ask, I think. But you would be surprised how easy it is to speak, and how difficult it is to listen."

"Perhaps," Marcus said. "What is it you wish to say?"

The highway replied, "Marcus. You are on a quest."

"I am?"

"You are," the highway solemnly replied.

"For what?" Marcus asked.

"To complete what you started."

"I am confused," Marcus confessed. "What did I start?"

"You will find out," the highway replied.

"Well... how am I to finish what I started if I don't know what I started?" Marcus exclaimed.

"You will see."

"Okay..." Marcus said, trailing off. "What do I do then?"

"Just keep doing what you are already doing."

"So... I'm on a quest to be myself for some great unknown reason?" Marcus asked. "And what is it I'm doing that I'm supposed to keep doing?!"

"You have much to learn," the highway replied. "You are a very unique person in this world."

"So... I guess this should be an easy quest then," Marcus said.

"No, no, no," the highway replied. It let out a sigh. "I'm afraid it will be quite long and draining. You'll need your strength, endurance, and courage. You'll need your strength of will."

"This does not make sense!" Marcus cried.

"The world rarely does," the highway said. "Just follow the road."

"Follow the road?" Marcus asked.

"Yes. Follow the road," the highway replied.

Marcus thought for a moment. "Is it a long way?"

"It is a very long way."

"Well... what is at the end, then?" Marcus asked.

"You will see... yes you will see," the highway said. "Just keep following. Keep following and I'll take you to the ones you loved. And I'll show you the world along the way."

13. Well Read in Not Theory

I watched the lane division lines scroll by. The flickering motion of the paint seeped into my mind. It almost felt like the highway wanted to tell *me* something.

We passed a rest stop. I hoped Sheridan didn't notice it, because I didn't want to admit my curiosity was piqued by the talking highway. It seemed like such a *stupid* story. Sheridan didn't look my way, but he was smiling slyly.

I bet he knew.

"Next one?" Sheridan asked.

"*How* do you keep reading my mind?" I asked.

Sheridan grinned. "What else would you be thinking?"

I hated to think I was that predictable. Sheridan was just playing mind-games with me. Perhaps... I didn't know. I stared at the road.

Sheridan was watching me stare at the highway. He said, "Roads are notorious for handing out difficult quests. In fact, it is well known the highway hands out the most difficult quests of all. Though, in Marcus's case, he had not a clue what his quest even was..."

- 11 -

Marcus sat by a brook which ran alongside the road. He stretched out and soaked his feet in its cool, refreshing water.

It was about ten feet across, and stretched as far as he could see. Every so often, a few cattails or rocks poked out, creating little ripples in the water. A few leaves and twigs floated downstream. In fact, the brook seemed to contain little bits and pieces of everything in the terrain.

"Hey!" a voice sounded.

Marcus looked around. At first, he thought the highway might be speaking again, but it sat silently.

"Down here!" it called.

He looked down at the water.

"Hi," the brook said.

"Hi... brook?" Marcus replied.

"Would you kindly remove your feet?"

Marcus was caught off guard - not by the brook's question, but that it was asking questions. For a moment, he wondered if he was losing his mind. He tried to lift his head with his hands, but confirmed it was still firmly attached to his neck. *I can't be losing my mind,* he thought. *For it is surely contained in my head, which is attached to my body.*

The brook was waiting patiently for Marcus's reply. He managed only a quick, quiet response, "Why?"

"It is quite clear you have traveled far..." the brook said. "... a little too clear."

Marcus pulled his feet from the water and stood up. "Sorry."

"No offense... really."

"Oh no, I understand! I wouldn't want someone's smelly feet on me either."

"Thank you for understanding. You are a gentleman," the brook replied. "It is not so much you, though. It is more the matter of maintaining a pleasant aroma."

"I was not aware such matters were of much concern," Marcus said. "At least... for a brook."

"On the contrary, good hygiene is very important!" the

brook exclaimed. "And one finds that when they keep a neat, tidy appearance, they are more likely to be taken seriously."

"Yes, that is true," Marcus said. "Perhaps I should pay better attention to my own presentation. I do wish to be taken seriously when I speak."

"As do I," the brook said. "But the fish! The fish do not do much to help my smell."

"Fish smell bad?" Marcus asked. "I mean... while they're alive and swimming?"

"Quite!" the brook exclaimed. "It is all I can do to maintain a pleasant aroma and appearance while fish are swimming inside me. Can you imagine the difficulties of maintaining good hygiene while hosting all sorts of aquatic life?"

Marcus thought for several moments before answering, "Honestly, I can't say I can."

"It is a wise man who is aware of what he does not know," the brook said. "I can assure you, though, it is quite unpleasant."

"I did not notice an offending odor," Marcus offered. "Although... I could not lean down to take a sniff without passing by my own feet. And I must confess, they are in need of a good washing."

"That is the problem with travel," the brook said. "It is quite lovely, but it doesn't do wonders for one's feet. I'm curious, why have you traveled so far?"

"The highway told me!" Marcus exclaimed. He shook his head. "And it is all so very confusing. I have a very long roll of paper. Is it my quest to fill it up?"

"That would be a silly quest," the brook replied, "Rather, I say it is *infinitely* long."

Marcus raised an eyebrow. "Infinitely long? I am rather sure I can only extend the paper so far."

"No," the brook said. "As soon as you reach the spindle, you simply desire more paper."

"So I'll never fill it up?"

"No."

"Then what is my quest?" Marcus exclaimed. He threw his arms in the air. "I need to know!"

"Perhaps your quest is to determine your quest," the brook said. "Often, knowing what to do is the hardest part of doing anything at all."

Marcus took a seat on a nearby tree stump. He stared into the water. "True," he said. "I have so little to go on."

"Don't feel bad," the brook said. "I imagine very few of us know where we are going. You'll figure it all out."

"Master Sophus told me to seek wisdom," Marcus said. "Perhaps... enough wisdom to determine my quest?"

The brook nodded. "But before you can learn what it is you should do, you must learn what it is you should *not* do."

"A wise man knows not what to do," Marcus said.

The brook corrected him. "A wise man knows *what not* to do. Every Mathematician should be well read in Not Theory."

"But how does one know what not to do without doing the things he is to not?" Marcus began to comprehend just how much his life had changed in a short time. He looked around, seeing the brook on both horizons.

"You have a lot to absorb. Perhaps this is why the highway told you to travel. Just travel. The answers will come."

Marcus looked down the road. "All roads lead to Rome," he said. "So perhaps I should go there... to the conference. Perhaps an answer will lie there."

"Perhaps."

Marcus peered down the road and smiled briefly - hopefully. "I'll give it a try," he said. "Thank you."

14. To Exist in Nothingness

Sheridan said, "So Marcus spent the next several hours trying to decide if he had gone completely insane."

"Of course," I said.

Sheridan grinned. "That's when things took a strange turn..."

- 12 -

As Marcus continued down the highway, he thought about the purpose of his journey. He contemplated that the whole point of the quest may just be to exist - so that he had some goal to seek while he gathered experience. The goal itself was not really a goal at all! It was just motivation.

Or perhaps he was wrong.

Frustrated, he stopped in the road, stretched his arms, and stared at the sky. He exclaimed, "Highway! Send me a sign!"

With his head in the clouds, he didn't notice he was in the path of a merchant's cart. Nearly struck by the galloping horses, he quickly jumped backward and fell into the bushes.

How ironic, he thought. *Or is it?*

Despite the scrapes and bruises, Marcus learned two things about wisdom from the encounter. Not looking where one is going is a bad idea, and wisdom implies knowledge of that fact, thus illustrating the irony in the necessity of making bad decisions in order to learn to make good ones.

Marcus wrote both lessons in his roll of paper and decided it was a very good start. He made a note in the margin concerning the proper use of "irony" and told the trees, "Good grammar will take you far in life!"

The trees swayed in the breeze, and Marcus imagined they were cursing him, as correcting another's grammar in conversation is terribly rude and nobody likes it.

Marcus went on walking and discussing irony with the trees. It was, for the most part, a one-sided conversation. The trees did nod and sway, acknowledging Marcus's existence. But they were still miffed about the grammar correction. Marcus shook his head and reminded them, "I really am sorry about that."

He was quite startled when he heard a woman's voice exclaim, "Good sir, why do you talk to the trees?"

Marcus collected his senses. "Do you think the trees have no interest in us?" He tapped the trunk of a tree.

The woman smiled. "Perhaps. Perhaps not. They do seem to be living perfectly happy despite our presence." She seemed strangely amused by the trees. "I'm Vasigari. And yes, I know who *you* are."

Marcus studied the stranger before him. Vasigari was tall, slender, with dark, unkempt hair and a perpetual sly smile. She wore a necklace with a small, silver fox paw, and carried what looked to be a long tiki torch. Yet, something about the fire seemed *off*. It took a moment of contemplation for Marcus to get it. No matter which angle he inspected it, the flames did not reflect on the necklace. He studied it for a good minute before he noticed Vasigari glaring icily at him. Perhaps she did not wish for people to so closely examine her trinket.

Marcus uttered the first excuse that came to mind - which

he immediately regretted - "Oh, pardon, I was just admiring your chest."

Vasigari smiled. "I like a man who is honest."

Marcus froze. He was trapped. For the situation was quite the opposite - he really *was* admiring the trinket. However, should he clarify, Vasigari would no longer think of him as "honest."

She laughed and shook her head. "And I wondered... just what the odds were that we would cross paths."

Marcus scratched his head. "I suppose the probability was greater than none, seeing as we stand before each other."

"You would think so," Vasigari said. "But I would go a step further and say it was precisely one."

"That's a decent chance."

Vasigari smiled. She leaned close to Marcus's ear and said, "*You* were worth the wait."

Marcus's eyes grew wide. Vasigari grinned. "I heard you make problems go away."

"Really?" Marcus asked. "Me?"

"You seem surprised," Vasigari replied. "Word travels fast. I was wondering if... perhaps... you'd be interested in helping me?"

Marcus thought for a moment, drawing out a hum. Vasigari added, "Of course, I'd be willing to compensate you." She leaned in close and said, "*Very* well."

Marcus gulped. Vasigari smiled slyly. "You can prove things don't exist, can't you?" she asked.

Marcus stood up straight and tightened his shoulders. "That *is* my specialty," he boasted.

"So if I were to ask you to *prove away* something," Vasigari said, "you could do it... being the great hero you are?"

"Of course," Marcus said. He bowed slightly. "I am at your service. Just tell me what it is you wish to be *proven away*, and I will get to work."

Vasigari wasted no time replying. "The world."

Marcus smiled and quickly agreed, "Certainly."

Vasigari grinned slightly and nodded. "Excellent."

Then the smile dropped from Marcus's face. "Wait."

"Yes?" Vasigari asked innocently.

"... the world..." Marcus said slowly. "... Hold on..."

"I am holding."

"Well..." Marcus said. He held up his thumb and finger, close together. "There is one minor... technical issue."

Vasigari sighed. "Isn't there always."

"Well... this reward..."

"You'll love it." Vasigari smiled suggestively.

Marcus continued, "If the world no longer exists, how am I to get it?"

"What do you mean?" Vasigari tilted her head slightly.

"What I mean is..." Marcus paused for a moment. "If the world no longer exists, neither do I."

"Why would you prove yourself away?" Vasigari asked. "That would be silly."

"Silly," Marcus repeated.

"Yes," Vasigari said. "Silly."

"But I am in the world."

"Yes."

"And if I prove the world does not exist," Marcus said, "then... how do *I* exist?"

For a moment, Vasigari said nothing. Marcus began to grow a little anxious waiting for her reply. Was she upset? Angry? He wasn't sure if she was the type to be tampered with. She then said, quietly, "I'm not sure."

"You're not *sure*?"

"I have never lived in a non-existent world before," Vasigari said. "Have you?"

"I see," Marcus said. "Me neither. So you see my concerns?"

"I see you're afraid of the unknown," Vasigari said.

"What?" Marcus said. He stood up straight. "No... no!"

"Yes... yes."

"No," Marcus replied. "It just seems to follow that, if what I exist in no longer exists, then *I* no longer exist."

"You think so, don't you?"

"Well..." Marcus said. "I have no proof -"

"And what is a Mathematician without his proof?" Vasigari asked. She smiled.

"Okay, okay," Marcus said. "Perhaps I should obtain proof."

"I want you to climb to the peak of The Mount of Mislor," Vasigari said. She nodded to herself.

"Which seems like a random request."

"*Pseudo*-random." Vasigari eyed Marcus sternly.

Marcus stared back blankly.

She then added, "At the top of the mountain you'll find Eru, the wise-man. If it will make you feel better, go see him first. *Then* you can start working on my request."

"...Ohh.. kay..," Marcus said, "I -"

"Excellent," Vasigari interrupted.

"I -" Marcus repeated. "Where did she go...?" He looked around. He saw only the forest shrubbery. He scratched his head.

For the rest of his walk, Marcus wondered if he had really agreed to the task of proving the world didn't exist.

15. **I Would Rather Exist**

There were too many idiot knuckleheads on the roads during the day. At night, the roads are quiet and empty.

Sheridan laughed. "If we all told our own stories, I'm sure someone out there would find it silly."

"But you can't make something go away just by proving it doesn't exist!"

"On the contrary," Sheridan said. "The nature of proof suggests otherwise."

"Wait... so you're saying you can point to me and *prove* that I don't exist?"

Sheridan nodded. "It would be very foolish of me to prove you do not exist, for the obvious reason that you are the one driving."

I wondered, and not for the first time, if Sheridan was making a good game of all these proofs. "Okay. I can play your game. The truck barreling toward us does not exist." I pointed to the empty road ahead. By this time, we were just shy of the state border. It was getting fairly late - the best time to be on the road.

I expected Sheridan would say something along the lines of "but there is no truck in front of us!" And I had my whole argument mapped out. But he only stared at me a brief moment, then said, "Any mathematician will tell you that proposing evidence is not quite the same as a proof."

"But there is no truck in front of us!" I exclaimed. "None.

Zilch!"

"And am I to accept that as true, given only what our eyes inform us is so?," Sheridan asked. "That is no proof!" He sure did seem to be enjoying himself. "The question of the *reason* for our existence is even more exasperating."

"More so than your conversations?" I asked.

Sheridan smiled. "It's a case of science and religion. Religion gives us a reason, but no proof. Science gives us a mechanism for proof, but no reason."

"So what do you do?" I asked.

Sheridan explained. "Well, these days, people just tune into the latest episode of *That's My Crazy Family! -*"

I chuckled. "I love that show!"

"- so they don't have to think about these things."

"Ah! But they had no television back then!" I said. "What did they do instead?"

Sheridan smiled again. "Let me tell you about when Marcus met Cisero."

- 13 -

Marcus strolled along the highway, cursing his poor fortune so far. He had only been out in the world a short time and already found himself on the task of eliminating his own existence.

He outlined his options. Prove the world didn't exist, and take himself out with it; prove the world didn't exist, and find himself in some unfathomable new existence; or shrug off Vasigari's request and face her wrath. He wasn't sure what kind of wrath Vasigari could bring, but she did not seem to be of the sort one should disappoint.

He threw his arms up in frustration. "Highway! Send me a sign!" he exclaimed.

He came to a fork in the road. The road sign pointed two different ways: "Mount of Mislor: 22; Rome: 94."

"And here lies the rub," he said to himself. "I asked the highway for a sign. It provided. And I still have to make a decision."

He looked down the two roads, and began to think of Master Sophus. For the first time since he left Ebon, he wished he could ask his advice. He stared at the clouds for a while as they sailed, drifting by quickly, phasing the sun's light in and out. They came in sizes - big, small, small, small, huge, big, huge, big, huge - and for a brief moment he saw the world with clarity. The once *random* sequence became *pseudo-random* and the world made sense. For a moment.

Marcus's eyes caught the sun and he turned away. He rubbed his eyes.

"Sir!" a man exclaimed.

Marcus jumped. He quickly turned about to find himself face-to-face with a fellow traveler. "Marcus!" the man exclaimed, smiling eagerly.

Marcus returned his smile and studied that man. He had wavy, blond hair and amber eyes - eyes which seemed to blend in with the lightly colored tree trunks. "Have we met?" he asked.

The man grinned and nodded enthusiastically. "In the village! When you told of your great accomplishment.

Marcus laughed. "Yes. Now I remember."

"My name is Cisero," he said with a slight bow of his head. "I am quite the fan of your work."

Marcus smiled. "Non-existence? It was nothing... really."

"Oh! Don't be so modest!" Cisero exclaimed. "Why... you have great things ahead of you!"

"I do?"

"Indeed," Cisero said. He nodded enthusiastically. "Your work is great. And great work should be shared.

"I am adept at non-existence proofs," Marcus said. He smiled.

"I must admit I am a bit nervous. You will not prove I don't exist, will you?"

"Why, of course not!" Marcus exclaimed.

Cisero smiled. "You are a true friend, then," he said. "Why, I bet you could prove the world itself doesn't exist!"

Marcus laughed. "Perhaps! It is funny that you mention that, because I just met someone who asked me to do that very task."

Cisero glanced into the horizon with a concerned stare. Marcus said, "But before I left Ebon, I had discussed proving quite the opposite with my master."

Cisero nodded. He smiled. "You should certainly prove we exist! Such a feat would be quite notable, indeed."

"I thought as much," Marcus said. "And given the choice of existing versus not, I would rather exist."

"Who wouldn't?"

"But, to be honest, both proofs are tricky," Marcus said. "It is in the nature of good Mathematics that at least one of the two states be established. I'm pretty sure my quest is to write one of these proofs."

"Pretty sure?" Cisero said.

"The highway told me I'm on a quest," Marcus said. "But it didn't say -"

Marcus paused, caught off guard by Cisero's grin. Cisero hid it. He said, "Continue."

"... it didn't say what it was."

"I see," Cisero said. "Let's walk... and let me explain who I am..."

Cisero lead Marcus away from the highway. They stopped on top of a small hill, surrounded by fields. From this modest peak, the surrounding villages could be seen, baking in the hot sun. Cisero watched them for a moment, then turned to Marcus. "I am the games-administrator of a little village known as Rome."

"Rome?" Marcus eagerly asked.

"I coordinate the great events," Cisero said. "Think of me as a publicity man. I'm your gateway to fame. Let's say... over a thousand years from now, what do you want people to think when they hear the name Marcus?"

"Good things, I would hope."

"But not nothing?"

"No!" Marcus said. "I would hope something! Well, not anything. Something *good*. I don't want to be *in*famous."

Cisero applauded. "So certainly you must agree to the merits of recognition for your own work." He motioned toward the villages in the fields. "Look at them," he said. "Imagine if they all knew you! Imagine if the whole countryside knew you!"

"It appears many do," Marcus said. He grinned.

Cisero grinned back. "They do! But... what about a hundred years from now? A thousand? Fifteen hundred?"

"I don't know."

"If your research is immortal, then you are immortal," Cisero explained. "And if you are immortal, your life will never be rendered meaningless."

"True," Marcus said. "That would be lovely."

"But you must make your research immortal," Cisero said, "It must stand up to peer review. There is a Conference in Rome."

Marcus interrupted. "Yes... as a matter of fact, I am headed that way now."

Cisero laughed. "My friend! You are going the wrong way."

Marcus kept his journey to see the wise-man to himself. He shrugged. "I just need something worthy of presenting. My late master... Master Sophus... told me to journey. Then I would know what to present."

"And you don't think proving the world exists would be worthy?"

Marcus stared at his hands for a moment. He then looked up. "Yes," he said. "Yes! Then I shall, indeed, solidify our existence."

"Why, such an accomplishment would double your reputation! Triple!" Cisero exclaimed. "Quadruple? N-tuple!"

"N-tuple my reputation, you say!" Marcus exclaimed.

Cisero nodded vigorously. "Yes, my friend.

Marcus said, "Well! I must say... this does sound marvelous. But why are you so eager to help me? Not that I mind! It's quite flattering, actually."

Cisero smiled. "It's my job!"

"What would I owe you for your efforts? I assume you would not work for free."

Cisero stood quietly for a moment. "Well... I usually charge 5,000 Denarii per 'N'. After subtracting one, of course."

"So... to double my reputation would be 5,000 Denarii."

Cisero nodded again.

Marcus shook his head. "That's a bit too rich for my blood."

"But, but, but!" Cisero exclaimed. "I'm an *agent*. And a reputable agent doesn't charge up front." He thought quietly for another moment. "We can work out financial matters after you write your proof. I've admired your efforts for quite some time, and you show promise! Prove the world exists... and I will make you famous!"

"You, indeed, are a good friend," Marcus said.

Cisero smiled slightly, then quickly faced the road.

- 14 -

As soon as Cisero left, Marcus bit his lip. He knew he was in trouble. Indeed, he'd been asked by Vasigari to do the exact opposite - prove the world did *not* exist - and he was fairly certain the world could not both exist and not exist.

He wondered what sort of wrath he could expect from Vasigari if he proved the world *did* exist, and wondered if, perhaps, he could reach a compromise. Existence for some, non-existence for others. He glanced at his roll of paper and shook his head. He then looked up at the sky.

"Master Sophus," he said. "I've really done it, now. Do I prove the world exists? Does not exist? I hope... oh I hope, the wise-man will grant me the wisdom to know which to do. Perhaps he'll explain to me how to make existence understandable."

16. The Other Daughter

Sheridan took a moment to stare at the billboards passing by. I wondered why he found them so fascinating. I was afraid to ask, but curiosity got the better of me.

Sheridan smiled. "If you exclude the 1-800 portion, the telephone numbers on the billboards, lined up, form the Fibonacci sequence."

I blinked, twice, in silence. Sheridan began to explain. "It's a string of numbers. The first two are ones. Each subsequent number is the sum of the previous two. 1, 1, 2, 3, 5, 8, 13, -"

"I've heard of it," I interrupted Sheridan.

Sheridan eyed me curiously. "You don't believe me? We can go back..."

I shook my head. "I believe you. It's just..." Sheridan continued to stare. I exclaimed, "*Who* notices these things!"

Sheridan laughed. "Nature contains many patterns..."

"I wasn't aware phone numbers grew in nature."

Sheridan said, "If life is like the wind's currents and water's ripples - then it should be of no shock at all."

I lifted an eyebrow. Sheridan nodded his head. "You'll see... in time. For now, let me tell you about the Idol of Trey..."

- 15 -

With the sun about to disappear, Marcus stopped at a small house along the road. Its sign read, "Elm's Inn and Nourishment for Travelers."

The house was almost entirely empty. Only two others, a young man and woman, were inside. Marcus sat down at one of the tables and continued thinking about his predicament. He asked himself what Master Sophus would advise, but in his head he could only picture the village children playing out the window.

He was interrupted by the woman. She was shorter than she initially appeared, and had light brown hair and eyes. The young man was much taller, with black hair and hazel eyes. They were smiling and eager to talk.

Marcus flashed a brief smile back and mumbled, "Hi."

He was not really in the mood to speak to anyone, but before he could say anything, the woman had already taken a seat.

"May we join you?" the man asked as he climbed into the other seat.

"Sure," Marcus replied. "But I must warn you that I'm not much of a conversationalist."

"That's okay," the man said. "I'm not much of a listener."

Marcus introduced himself.

"I'm Aspen," the man said. "And this is my wife, Utica."

Utica smiled at Marcus. "Why are you traveling?"

"I'm on a quest," Marcus said. "But I don't know why... or for what."

"Sounds intriguing," Utica said. "We have a reason, but no quest."

Marcus lifted an eyebrow. "How can one have a reason without a quest?"

"Because it is good," Aspen said. "That is the reason...

but I'm not sure *why*."

Utica added, "That's how Eru, the wise-man, explained it to us."

"Our parents disapprove of our love," Aspen said. "So we went to see Eru... hiked right up that mountain. It was a grueling climb. And no sooner had he seen us, than he said, 'You should act because it is the good thing to do.' "

"We asked him what, exactly, was good?" Utica said. She sighed. "And he said..."

Aspen interrupted. " 'Good is an adjective used to describe something that is morally right.' "

Utica said, "Then I asked... 'How do I know that which is morally right?' "

Aspen said, "And he replied, 'First determine that which is morally left, then go the other direction.' "

Utica held her face in her hand and shook her head.

Marcus stared out the window for a moment. Barely visible, and far in the distance, was the faint outline of the Mount of Mislor. He wondered if Eru knew he was coming. "I'm on my way to see Eru, myself."

"Good luck," Utica said. She tried to hide a snicker.

Aspen said, "Well, I read in *The Philosophy* about advice -"

Utica rolled her eyes. Marcus asked, "Philosophy?"

Aspen glared at Utica. She explained, "*The Philosophy of Many Hands*. He's always quoting it."

"So what does the... *Philosophy* say about advice?" Marcus asked.

Utica rolled her eyes again - in the other direction. Aspen smiled and, in a clear, loud voice, stated: " 'Advice is like beans boiling in a pot over fire - the steam likely smells like beans.' "

Utica groaned. Aspen said, "I, for one, happen to think it's a *wonderful* philosophy." He nodded to himself.

"It sure hasn't helped us much," Utica said. "Here we

are... without direction. We can't go home... and we have nowhere else to go."

"But you!" Aspen exclaimed. "You have a quest! For what?"

"I don't know!" Marcus threw his arms in the air.

Utica tapped her fingers on the table as she thought. "Then I suppose, first, it is a quest for wisdom."

Marcus bit his lip as he thought this through. "Explain?"

"Well," Utica explained, "Many think wisdom means knowing it all. But the wise man knows that one can't know *everything*. So wisdom must be knowing the right questions to ask."

Marcus thought this was a very wise observation. In particular, he liked that it did not rule out the possibility of him becoming wise himself. "I could use more wisdom," he replied.

He flashed his roll of paper. "It is infinitely long," he explained. "No matter how much I learn, I will never fill it up."

Utica smiled. "That doesn't mean you shouldn't write at all. What should you start filling it with?"

"I'm on my way to a conference," Marcus said. "My master told me to learn something, then present it. But he didn't like my original research. I was going to present my non-existence proof... the one I used to slay the Giant Dachy."

"Wait!" Utica exclaimed. "What did you say your name was?"

"Marcus," Marcus said. "Marcus Numus Tullis."

Aspen laughed. "Well, well!"

"We've heard of you!" Utica said. "Quite an extraordinary achievement. Non-existence proofs can be quite tricky... or so I've heard."

Marcus nodded. "I think you were right about a quest for wisdom," he said. "Perhaps there is something to learn from my current predicament. You see, I stand at a cross-road. To prove the world exists. Or to prove the world does not exist." He explained his encounter with Vasigari and Cisero.

Utica nodded. "To be honest, I wouldn't know where to begin with *either*."

"Non-existence, in particular, is difficult," Marcus said. "It is easy to see what is, for what *is* in existence is that which you see. But what is in non-existence... is difficult to see, because what you don't see may be non-existent, or may exist, but lie unseen, you see?"

Utica said, "I see. I see what I saw, but not that which I've never seen."

Marcus said, "So the proof that what you don't see is never to be seen is difficult to concoct. But trickier is the proof that what you *do* see is *not*."

"But you have the proof!" Aspen exclaimed. "I have heard you have quite the sense of the Non."

"Yes," Marcus said. "I am quite full of Non-sense."

Utica and Aspen exclaimed in unison, "Indeed!"

Utica said, "Oh! I hope you don't prove we do not exist!"

"I wouldn't do that," Marcus said. "Just the world was all that was requested of me."

From behind the counter, someone exclaimed, "I'd very much like to keep my inn, too!"

Aspen laughed. A man, tall, old, with gray hair and gray eyes, poked his head out of the doorway.

"That's Elm," Utica explained. She waved.

"Yes," Elm said. "And I've worked too hard to have some wise-guy prove my work doesn't exist."

"Oh shush," Aspen said. "He wouldn't do that!"

Utica smiled reassuringly. "He's too much of a gentleman."

"Indeed," Marcus said.

"Nevertheless," Aspen said. "Between you and I and the

whole mess our world has been recently... perhaps it *would* be best to prove it away."

"Don't you prove my inn away!" Elm exclaimed. He raised his walking stick.

"No, sir," Marcus said. "I shall write a list. A list of things to keep."

And under the heading *THINGS TO KEEP* Marcus wrote:

1. Myself... Marcus

2. Utica

3. Aspen

4. Elm

5. Elm's inn

Aspen looked over Marcus's shoulder. "And there's this particular kind of cheese I like. It has a fluffy texture. And it's soft."

Marcus nodded. He jotted down:

6. Some kind of fluffy cheese.

Utica rolled her eyes. "You and your cheese. Nevermind the works of the great philosophers. The great writers. The great heroes. They don't matter, for in this new world, we shall have *cheese!*"

Aspen leaned back with wide eyes. "New world?"

Utica said, "If this world no longer exists, we shall exist *somewhere.*" She looked at Marcus. "Wouldn't we?"

Marcus shrugged. Aspen bit his lower lip. "I don't know what is out there... maybe this is a bad idea."

Marcus looked Aspen's way. "Shall I, instead, prove the world *does* exist? It's bad mathematics to have a world which is not proven one way or the other."

Elm whacked Marcus on the head. "You leave my inn be!"

Marcus cried out, jumped up, and swiped Elm's stick. Aspen laughed. Elm warned, "There's plenty more of those where that one came from."

Marcus threw his hands in the air. "Okay!" he said.

Aspen interrupted, laughing. "Perhaps!" he exclaimed. "Perhaps the idol will help you make sense of all this."

Utica rolled her eyes.

Marcus raised an eyebrow. "What idol?"

Aspen nodded. "Surely you, coming from Ebon, are aware of the Idol of Trey."

Marcus nodded. "Ah! Indeed, I bet that would grant the wisdom to know what to do."

"It'd grant you wisdom to know how many sticks I have in the back," Elm said. He swiped the one back from Marcus. Marcus stared at his empty hands.

"Oh... that's all silly," Utica said. "For one thing, The Idol of Trey *is* a legend... Is it even real?"

Marcus opened his mouth, but Aspen quickly interrupted. "But this is *Marcus*! Let's say it isn't real. If he can prove something that is *does not* exist, then perhaps he could prove something that is not *does*!"

Marcus held his forehead and shook his head.

"I'll see it when I believe it," Elm said.

Utica said, "He'll *believe* it when he *sees* it."

Elm shook his head. Utica smiled. She stuck her tongue out at Aspen. "Perhaps he could just obtain the idol and let *it* tell him how to prove it exists."

"Oh good lord," Marcus interrupted. "Perhaps I need the idol just to make sense of you."

Utica smiled.

- 16 -

Marcus sat on the inn's front lawn with Utica and Aspen, watching the sky. The day had ended and left a full sky of stars as a parting gift. He enjoyed star-gazing. He recalled the happy days of his childhood, spent attempting to learn the constellations. He never did learn them very well. And it was only as far back as the start of his teenage years that he had finally realized *different* stars came out at night, depending on the season.

"There are a lot of stars up in the sky," Aspen said.

"Certainly so," Marcus replied. "Why, I can see Aries the lamb!"

Utica giggled. "That's ram."

Aspen poked Marcus in the rib. "It's okay."

Marcus eyed the sky again. "And there is Taurus, the donut."

"It's a bull!" Utica laughed. "Don't you know the sky?"

"Hey! Okay, I admit... I don't know much about it!" Marcus exclaimed. He squinted, failing to grasp how the donut-shaped constellation formed a bull.

"Here, I'll teach you," Utica said. "See the North Star?"

Marcus nodded.

"Look just to the right. There is a line of four stars that form a little arch. See it?" Utica asked.

"Yes, I think so," Marcus replied.

"Do you see the two stars just below the arch? One to the left of the middle, and one to the right?" Utica asked.

"Maybe... Yes! I see it!" Marcus exclaimed.

Utica answered, "Well, to the right of the arch are three stars that form a small triangle."

"Yes..." Marcus said.

Utica added, "That's Trey."

"Trey?" Marcus asked. 'The dachshund?"

"The great *flying* dachshund!" Utica exclaimed. "A flying dachshund who watches over the interests of those who are curious about the world and nature."

Marcus squinted as he studied the pattern. Eventually, yes! There *was* a dachshund constellation.

"Trey is very kind and benevolent. He is also very wise," she continued

"A wise wiener dog?" Aspen asked. "You've never told me that before."

"I've told you there was a dog up there!" Utica exclaimed. "I told you the day we hosted that silly gathering. Remember? You were all upset about the custard and its ill-fated flight... and then we made up when we watched the sky together."

Aspen grumbled. "I *told* you that the table had a missing leg and might collapse!"

"Well, I'm sorry!" Utica said. "We needed it..."

Marcus coughed and cleared his throat.

Utica poked his rib. Aspen changed the subject. "Having come from Ebon, I assume you know the story of the good sons and daughters."

"Parts," Marcus said. "The problem is that there are multiple versions of the story, and they all seem to contradict each other in little ways."

"Example?" Utica said.

Marcus stared at the Trey constellation. "I've been gathering the various versions of the story for years. The only thing anyone knows for sure is what was recorded in the minutes... a group of the village's sons and daughters were sent on a quest and never returned. But, there's no guarantee the minutes are factual."

"So there's nothing," Aspen said.

Marcus shook his head. "There was a child in the village. He was intrigued by the legend and spent quite a few afternoons in the library researching all about it. I never caught his name, but his house faced my tower. Many nights, I would catch him staring at it. One day, I ran into him at the market. I asked him what he found so fascinating about it. He really, really wanted my job."

Marcus looked up at the constellation again. "One day he told me about The Temple of the Night Song. Everyone knows about the Idol, but nobody knows about the Temple."

Aspen shook his head. "I've never heard about it."

Marcus said, "A few days after the lockdown started, a small group of the children - four of the sons, and four of the daughters - approached the council hall. They told of a group of monks, *The Temple of the Night Song*, who had sent for them. The children said that the monks heard of their peril. They claimed to have a remedy. But the good sons and daughters were to come at once."

"And I suppose the idol was the remedy?" Utica asked.

Marcus nodded. "The idol would grant the wisdom to know how to defeat the Giant Dachy. The elders sent the sons and daughters to go find the idol. Or take it to the monks. Or... well, its existence at the time is dubious. But *that* was the quest... the one that was omitted from the minutes."

"Well," Aspen said. "The legend around *here* is what happened to the *daughters*."

"No sons?" Marcus asked.

"Well, they split," Aspen said. "I mean... they were free! To do what they pleased! Most of them didn't care what they did after leaving. They went to have fun -"

"Presumably to die," Utica said.

Aspen said, "Well, nobody knows. They must have left for Rome. But, two of the daughters still had the idol."

"Hence, their fate," Utica added.

"What happened?" Marcus asked.

"The oldest... Ilia," Aspen said. "now exists nowhere."

Utica added, "and the youngest, I forgot *her* name, now exists everywhere."

"How do you exist *everywhere*?" Marcus asked. "I've been around here and there by now... but one thing I know is that I'm certainly not everywhere at once."

"You'd have to ask her," Aspen said. He looked Utica's way and reminded her, "Her name was Vasigari."

17. The Problem With Infinities

The flickering of the passing streetlights was just flashy enough to give me a horrible headache.

Sheridan was his usual self. "It's like hurdling down the light corridor." Perhaps his grin was a bluff. Perhaps he was grinning because I was so wrapped up in figuring him out.

The car tires struck the little *thump thump thump thump thump thump thump thump* grooves. Sheridan quickly shook his head, laughed, and said, "*So*... The next day, Marcus began his journey to the wise-man's temple. He started hours before sunrise and had been hiking through the dawn. The heat was just starting to get to him..."

- 17 -

Marcus stood at the bottom of the mountain, looking up. The very top was obscured by a humid mist. He broke a sweat simply thinking about the hike to come.

How ridiculous my life has become! He shook his head as he glanced across the trail. *Here I am, on a quest without definition, on my way to see a wise-man for advice I don't want, concerning a job I don't want to do - that may or may not have even been assigned. I might as well prove the world doesn't exist and be done with it!*

Marcus pulled out the roll of paper Master Sophus had

given him. He shook his head again. *No. It would be much too difficult to fill the roll of paper in a world that doesn't exist.*

Tiny bright dots danced over the page. The spectacle caught Marcus off guard, and he wondered if the heat was starting to get to him. He looked up. The sun's rays flickered as the breeze swept through the tree leaves. He looked at the paper again. For a brief moment, the chaotic sequence of jumps made perfect sense - left, right, up, right, right, right, down, down, right - and the world itself came into focus.

Marcus shook his head again and saw nothing but chaos. He squinted to shield his eyes from the bright sunlight. After taking a moment to collect his senses, he wiped a sweat bead from his forehead, took a deep breath, and resumed his hike. He should, at least, hear what the wise-man had to say.

- 18 -

Hours later, Marcus stopped to rest. The sun had gained significant height and baked the trail to a light toast. Further up, the ground seemed to wobble. For a while, he wondered if the trail was wagging its tail. Perhaps not many people came this way.

He took a moment to sit in the shade. When he sat, he felt a bump. He reached down and pulled out Master Sophus's roll of paper. He twiddled it in his hand and thought, *Is what I learn a result of who I am, or is who I am the result of the wisdom I've obtained?*

He wrote, "I don't know," as his response. He decided it was a good response, because, as good responses should be, it was true.

"Marcus," someone whispered.

Marcus blinked and looked around. "Who is it?" he asked. "Who is speaking my name?"

"Many times, in life, there are questions," the voice said. "And on occasion, there may even be an answer!"

"I find it rather odd to be talking to nobody."

"And nobody finds it odd to be talking to you."

"But, are you nobody?"

"If I'm nobody," the voice said, "then I find it odd to be talking to you."

"*Do* you find it odd to be talking to me?" Marcus asked.

"No."

Marcus smiled. "Well, then... you're not *nobody*."

The voice applauded. "It's the contrapositive. I'm behind the bushes."

Marcus looked off to the side of the trail where the brook ran alongside. "Are you the brook?" he asked.

"Indeed I am!" the brook exclaimed. "And how happy I am that you recognized me."

"Of course," Marcus said. "Who else would know the proper difference between *contrapositive* and *converse*."

"That makes a brook happy," it said. "For I would much rather be known for proper identification of logical laws than the smell of the fish which swim in my waters."

"I would imagine we all would," Marcus said. "It is the mark of a good Mathematician, he who is more renowned for his proofs than his smell. Nobody remembers Archimedes's body odor."

"It has been much too long since we have conversed."

Marcus hung his head. "Perhaps it was the fault of the plumbing that I didn't need to leave the inn to receive water."

"Cursed aqueduct," the brook said. "But tell me... have you stayed true to your determination to fill the infinite roll?"

Marcus stared at the paper again. "You told me it was silly to try to fill it! That's the problem with infinities. I'd keep writing and writing, but be no closer to filling the roll than before I started."

"That doesn't mean you shouldn't *desire* to fill it," the brook said. "Perhaps that is the boon. For if the roll were finite, you would have to stop learning."

"I suppose," Marcus said. He glanced at the mountain peak. "You are wise, brook."

"Thank you."

"Where does your wisdom come from?"

"I am water, and water is ancient and wise."

Marcus bit his lip as he thought. "So maybe I should just drink some water?"

The brook laughed. "No! Silly human. There is no key to wisdom. You just keep learning about the world in which you stand. And never become so cocky as to think you have learned everything. When you stop learning, you are no longer wise."

Marcus carefully examined his roll of paper.

"So wisdom is an endless paper tape?" Marcus asked. He turned the roll of paper over in his hand.

"Yes," the brook replied. "Fill it up, segment by segment, with what you've learned. And what you've learned will then become the basis for how you perceive future experiences, and hence, the next lesson to be learned. Given enough time, you will have had enough experiences and enough lessons that your paper will contain much wisdom!"

Marcus thought about the brook's words.

The brook said, "I am long, and ancient as man himself. Hence, I have recorded volumes of wisdom... the cumulative knowledge of mankind."

"You are very long indeed," Marcus said. "But I am only a few feet tall and quite frustrated with the lack of details I received from the highway about this quest."

The brook said, "You can figure it out."

"I suppose," Marcus said. "Vasigari said to ask the wise-man about existence. Perhaps if I understood existence, I could figure out how to make it understandable?"

"I think..." the brook said. "... I think if you can answer *that* question, then it already is."

- 19 -

Marcus gazed toward the wise-man's house. It stood atop a short stone base, with four columns on each corner holding up the roof. The exterior walls reached two-thirds to the base of the ceiling, which provided the structure with ample light and space for the cool mountain breeze.

Marcus walked up to the doorway. There was no door - just an open space through which the wise-man watched Marcus. He smiled slightly and announced, "I've been waiting for you."

Marcus took a step back. "Me?"

"I don't see anybody else here," the wise-man said. "And I should know. I have eyes with which to see, ears with which to hear, and a mouth with which to keep shut so as not to impede the function of the aforementioned two parts."

Marcus nodded. "You are a very wise man. But how do you know who I am?"

The wise-man bowed his head slightly. "You seek recognition for your efforts. And that which you sought, you are on your way to having fulfilled. The question is, is what you seek what you really want?"

Marcus stared blankly at the man.

He continued, "Please, tell me what you wish to know."

Marcus had but one question for the wise man. "How do I make existence understandable?"

"Anything is understandable once you can understand it."

Marcus eyed the wise-man.

The wise man nodded. "The suffix *able*, appended to a verb, means the action described by the verb can be done."

Marcus scratched his head.

The wise man continued, "In general, suppose X is a verb. If you want it to be Xable, you need to X it."

Marcus's eyes grew wide as it clicked. "I see!" he exclaimed. "So if, for example, I want a mountain to be scalable, then I need to scale it."

"Exactly!" the wise-man said. "Or if something needs to be runnable -"

"It needs to run," Marcus finished.

"Ours is a fascinating language, isn't it?"

Marcus smiled. "Indeed."

Marcus then bid farewell to the wise-man and headed off. It was not until he finished his descent that he realized the understanding of existence would be an infinite quest - for he had received superb advice, but was no closer to understanding existence than before he began his trek.

18. Zero Percent Filled

"I think I would be pretty pissed if I hiked all the way up a mountain just to be told that *able* is a suffix," I said.

Sheridan smiled. "Are you suggesting it is not true?"

"Just because it's true doesn't mean it's good advice," I said. "I mean... gee... any idiot with half a brain can state obvious things and call it advice. The sky is blue!"

Sheridan quietly looked up at the sky. It was black.

"Don't even say it," I said.

"My lips are sealed."

I continued to smirk. Sheridan nodded. He said, "So, Marcus headed back to the inn..."

- 20 -

Marcus abruptly stopped in the trail. Faintly, he could hear singing. A tall wall of shrubs partitioned the road from the voice. Marcus placed his hand on the wall as the singing continued. *Who are you?* he thought. He leaned his ear against the shrubbery.

Marcus could not make out the words, but it was the sweetest voice he had ever heard; he had to find its source. He felt around the shrubs until he found a split. Carefully pulling the bushes apart, he formed a little opening and poked his head through. On the other side stood a girl. She stood in an empty field, singing the unrecognizable song as she dropped seeds into little trenches.

Marcus watched her for a moment. She had dark brown eyes that blended with the field in which she worked. Her long, deep crimson hair drifted in the breeze. He closed his eyes and let the song fill his mind.

He lost his footing and rustled the leaves.

The girl looked up at the bush and gasped. Marcus blinked, startled by her reaction. "Are you... a bush-man?" the girl asked.

Marcus shook his head. Leaves fell out of his hair.

"You look like a bush," the girl said. She smiled. "And a nervous one at that."

Marcus blushed as he carefully stepped out into the field. "I was... just on the road..." he said.

The girl smiled as he continued, "... and I heard you singing."

She blushed and said, "Oh dear... it is just a silly song! I didn't think anyone could hear."

"Oh no! You.. I mean it!.. is quite captivating," Marcus said.

The girl smiled. "I'm Peoria."

"What were you singing?" Marcus asked.

Peoria sang, "Close your eyes, sweet dreamer."

Marcus smiled at her.

"It's part of a lullaby," Peoria explained.

"You have a beautiful voice."

Peoria smiled. "Thanks. I only know those first five words, though."

Marcus raised an eyebrow. "Really? It sounded like you were singing more."

"I just sing the same five words over and over," Peoria replied. She grinned. "Every verse, though, is a different order of the words."

Peoria closed her eyes and sang, "Close your eyes, sweet dreamer... close your eyes, dreamer sweet... close your sweet, eyes dreamer..." She then laughed. "I learned it when I was little. I counted... there are 120 verses in all."

"Very... permutatoric," Marcus said.

Peoria asked, "So tell me... Marcus? What do you do?"

"Oh! I'm a mathematician!"

"Oh my! A regular Euclid!" Peoria exclaimed. "How unusual! What was your name again?"

"Marcus Numus Tullis."

Peoria gasped. "You are quite famous!"

"I am?"

"Yes!" Peoria said. "Until you, no one around here really believed the Giant Dachy were real. But you proved they exist!" She clapped her hands. "How exciting to meet a hero!" She squinted, glanced left and right, and said quietly, "Are you hunting more of them now?"

"I... " Marcus said. "I went to see Eru, the wise-man. I asked him how to make existence understandable."

"He is a very wise man."

"I don't doubt that," Marcus said. "Yet... I feel just as lost as before."

Peoria frowned. Marcus said, "But I met two travelers who told me the legend of an idol -"

"Oh!" Peoria exclaimed. "The idol that grants infinite wisdom! It is quite well known around here... Do you think you can find it?"

Marcus sighed. "I'm starting to think it is my only hope. So far, the only significant thing I have is a lesson in grammar, out of all my travels and experiences."

Marcus showed Peoria his infinite roll of paper. "So while I have *something* written down, I have zero *percent* filled."

Peoria poked Marcus. "Well... if the idol grants infinite wisdom... perhaps it would fill the infinite roll!"

"Oh my!" Marcus exclaimed. "You may be right."

Marcus thought, *With the idol, I would then have both an arbitrary large volume of knowledge, and an arbitrarily large volume of memory. It seems one can always count the number of things they've learned, but never the number of things they haven't learned. Mankind shall be doomed if the universe is expanding faster than he can learn, for our best philosophers will then be rendered infinitely stupid.*

"You are quite remarkable, Marcus." Peoria smiled.

"Thank you."

Peoria blushed.

19.   She's Been Watching You

We began to head down into another dip. Sheridan had taken a moment to think about... who knows what. In the distance, I could spot a billboard. "What's the next number in the Fibonacci sequence?" I asked.

"Well, it depends on where we started," Sheridan said.

"The billboards," I said. "Remember? You said the phone numbers formed the sequence."

Sheridan nodded. "I think it ended in 987, 1597... so the next would be 2584, 4181, 6765 -"

I nodded. I didn't know what Sheridan meant about life being something like the wind. But I did fear that I would never hear the end of it if Sheridan thought he was on to something. I held my breath.

The board read, "Carolina-Virginia Transport Co. 1-800-551-4906."

I breathed a sigh of relief. "Your pattern is broken," I said.

Sheridan lifted an eyebrow. Then his eyes lit up. "Oh! Yes. It's a new pattern now. The next number will be 8,504,906."

Sure enough, the next phone number was 1-800-850-4906.

"You've been down this road before," I said. That didn't really make it any more believable. Did he memorize every phone number along the route? I looked toward Sheridan. He had a sly smile. "Or," I said. "Perhaps you have the idol that grants infinite wisdom."

Sheridan said. "Does such an idol exist?"

"Marcus seems to think so."

Sheridan paused for a moment. "It certainly was on his mind..."

- 21 -

Marcus exclaimed, "You should come away with me! See the sights! See the cities!"

Peoria sighed. "I'm not allowed to stray far... I'm tied to the land."

"How are you tied?" Marcus asked. "You do not have bindings."

Peoria explained, "That doesn't mean I am free. I am a slave." She stared at the ground, watching the wind push the fallen leaves.

Marcus took her hand, and she looked up, smiling slightly. "I suppose I could move about some... if I don't go too far."

"Why... there's a lot right here, just waiting to be explored!" Marcus said. He plucked a leaf off of a nearby tree. He smiled at Peoria, holding up the leaf. "Look at its intricacies! I bet there is a whole world in there."

Peoria carefully examined all corners of the leaf. The pattern of the veins reminded her of the roads she'd traveled when she was younger - before she worked in the field. "Can you fit a whole world in a little pattern?"

Marcus shrugged. "I am not sure. That would be something, though."

Peoria carefully placed the leaf back onto the branch, hoping it would stick. "I never really paid attention to them. They are quite complicated... fascinating up close."

"Lately I have been seeing..." Marcus said. Peoria stared anxiously. Marcus scratched his head and said, "*patterns*."

"Patterns..." Peoria said quietly.

Marcus nodded. He told her that on his way to the wise-man he saw the sun's rays flicker. "They move so randomly," he said. "But for a moment... a brief moment... it all made sense. I knew the pattern."

Peoria smiled. "Maybe you have good intuition."

"Maybe that is the highway's quest. Perhaps it wishes me to find the answer... and explore -"

"The world!" Peoria exclaimed. "Wisdom encompasses the world! And if I could come with you, I could be a part of it, too."

"Then I will take you!" Marcus exclaimed. "Someday. Somehow, we will go on a quest for wisdom together."

"You *must* promise!" Peoria exclaimed. "Promise to take me on your quest. To take me exploring."

"I will," Marcus said. He smiled and nodded. "Someday! Someday I will.

"I think I would rather like to be a philosopher!" Peoria laughed and swirled herself about. "Oh! What things could I do without these chains? Without them, I would be a bird. I could soar!"

Marcus wished he could free Peoria. He saw in her a sharp mind and a kind heart. He wondered, *Is Peoria attached to strings as is the puppet?*

The clouds began to drift away. Peoria closed her eyes as the sun washed over her face. "I'll have wings," she said. "And I'll fly. You'll lift me off the ground and take me away."

Marcus smiled. "How wonderful a thought. Free to join me, if you wish, on my travels. Free to reach for the things in life you desire."

She continued to stare at the sky. She said, "We could meet Olive -"

Marcus lifted an eyebrow. "Olive?"

Peoria giggled. "Of the leaves." She glanced down the road. "It's a story I heard when I was little."

"Oh!" Marcus exclaimed. "*Do* tell!"

"I suppose we have time," Peoria said. She smiled. "It's about the sky... and the leaves..."

- 22 -

Marcus hesitated as he walked toward the master's house. He tried to determine why he was nervous. He was the great Marcus, defeater of the Giant Dachy.

Peoria's master was tall, over-bearing, and beefy. His frame filled the doorway when he answered Marcus's knock. His breath smelled like a cow when he grinned. He glared at Marcus, and muttered, "What?"

Marcus stood straight, shoulders back, and clearly said, "Peoria."

The master stared blankly. "Who?"

Marcus pointed toward Peoria. "Her... in the fields."

"Oh," the master said. "Yes. She helps me ready the fields."

"I would..." Marcus paused, thinking exactly how one words such a request. "I need... *an assistant*."

"Ohhhhh," the master said. He chuckled. "You wish to *purchase* her from me."

"Yes."

The master stroked his chin. "Tell ya what. After the crops are seeded..." He eyed Peoria again. "I'll let her go. Five-hundred Denarii."

"Wonderful," Marcus said. He tried to hide any emotion. "It's a deal!"

The master grinned again. "She's been watching you the whole time, you know."

"I... didn't notice," Marcus said. He shifted his eyes away for a moment.

The master burst out laughing. "Ah! Ha! Ha! You don't need an *assistant*."

Marcus diverted his eyes again. The master laughed more. "'Cause I just remembered. She's the only one who drops those seeds *just right*."

Marcus stared blankly. The master paused a moment, then said, "Fifty-thousand Denarii."

"Fifty-thousand!" Marcus exclaimed. "I thought we had a deal."

The master smiled. "Now we have a new deal. Fifty-thousand. No less."

"I... don't have that kind of money," Marcus said.

"Then you'd better go get it, huh?" the master asked. He slammed the door.

Marcus stopped the door with his hand. "I have another *proposition*."

The master folded his arms across his chest. "Let's hear it."

Marcus quietly offered the first valuable thing that came to mind. "The idol."

He regretted saying it as soon as he finished speaking.

"The *idol*?"

"Let's... barter," Marcus explained. "Surely you've heard of it! The idol that grants its bearer infinite wisdom."

The master said, "Yes. I've heard of *that*. You want to barter a story?"

"No, no," Marcus said. "It's real."

"Is that so?" the master asked. "Then where is it?"

"Well..." Marcus said. He mentally kicked himself.

The master chuckled. "I think I'd rather have the money, anyway." He started to slam the door.

Marcus stopped it again. "Wait, though. Think about it. Infinite wisdom."

"What do I need wisdom for?"

"It'll grant you the wisdom to get *more* money," Marcus said. "Think about it... would you rather have money... or the wisdom to get many, many monies?"

The master cracked a grin. "I suppose you have a point, there. *If* it is real."

"It *is* real. And I know where to find it," Marcus said. He lied - but the master need not know that.

"Let's see it, then," the master said. "Let's see it. Then we will talk."

"Okay."

Marcus began to turn away when the master called, "Hold it! Until you have it..." he said. *"Don't* let me catch you on my lands."

The master then promptly slammed the door. Marcus stared at it for a moment. He realized he had, quite possibly, made yet another big mistake.

As he wandered down the highway, he threw his arms in the air. *I am to prove the world does not exist while I also seek to prove it does. Now I must retrieve an idol which may or may not exist in a world which may or may not!*

Marcus sighed. He stared toward Peoria's field. It dawned on him that all he knew about the idol was that it was somewhere in the world. On the plus side, it *was* somewhere in the world. "I suppose that does narrow it down," he said. "How big could the world be?"

III
The Edge of Existence

20. A Pseudo-Random Request

The clouds were really freaking me out. Long, slender, claw-like tentacles reached down like a hundred anxious demons reaching for a victim. I recognized the formations.

When I was little, I lived in Texas for a few years. I recognized them from the day a tornado struck our town. The storm mostly spared the town, but shook everyone up nevertheless. The next year, my family moved to North Carolina and I hadn't seen the formations since.

But a tornado didn't seem right. It had stopped raining entirely, and the wind was almost non-existent. Maybe it was Sheridan's fault.

Something about Sheridan made me jumpy. Perhaps it was his demeanor. He commanded attention, and seemed to manipulate me into thinking about the things he wanted me to. The sky hadn't bothered me until I picked him up. His words, "the world is coming to an end", bounced around in my head. He seemed so care-free. *Too* care-free. And when I was with him, the world seemed so *strange*.

"From time to time," Sheridan said, "Marcus got caught up in nature's patterns..."

- 23 -

Marcus began to list in his head all the possible ways in which one could exist so that he could prove each did not apply to the master. He then paused. "If I prove the master doesn't exist," he said to himself. "And Peoria is his slave... does she not exist in turn?"

Marcus scratched his head. He continued on his way through the woods. He came upon a clearing which had three distinct paths. A heavy gust of wind came from the first. He could hear the trinkle of water from the second. The third appeared to lead to a mess of even more paths. He decided to avoid the third for now, and chose the first.

Marcus entered a windy clearing. Leaves soared and hovered about. He walked a bit further and noticed the wind scattering seeds as well. *This must be how the forests are formed*, he thought.

He stared at the rustling leaves for several moments, wondering if the way they danced in the breeze suggested an order. *Down, right, left, right, up, right,...* Marcus thought. He could not immediately fathom a pattern, but found it curious nonetheless.

"So," a female voice said.

Marcus jumped. He quickly turned around to find himself face-to-face with Vasigari. She smirked as she gazed around her, then eyed Marcus. "I woke up this morning, looked around, and said to myself, 'this still exists,' " she said.

Marcus collected his senses. "Of course it still exists!" he said. "Could you have thought otherwise? If there was no world to think in?"

Vasigari shook her head. "I was curious how you have been coming along with our deal?"

Marcus said, "I wasn't aware we finished discussing it."

Vasigari folded her arms in front of her chest and glared at Marcus. She sternly reminded him, "I believe your exact words were '...ohh... kay..' "

"Yes," Marcus said. "But... doesn't that seem hesitant to you?"

"It's not how you say it," Vasigari said. "It's what you said. Have you seen the wise-man? Didn't you go see Eru about the proof?"

"I did..."

"And he didn't help you?"

"Well...," Marcus said.

Vasigari's eyes grew wider with anticipation of the result. Marcus continued, "He told me, 'the suffix *able*, appended to a verb, means the action described by the verb can be done.' "

Vasigari smiled. "He is a very wise man."

"I'm not quite sure it's helpful advice - for I am no closer to having my answer than before I asked."

Vasigari nodded to herself and said, "There's an old proverb Eru gave me... it goes something like... 'A journey of a thousand miles begins with a council whose task is to instruct the traveler where to take the first step.' "

Marcus nodded. "Well, he is a very wise man."

"And yet," Vasigari said. "You're still stuck! Perhaps you are not the mathematician you claim to be."

"No, no," Marcus objected. "It's just difficult. The brook said if I could answer the question of how to make existence understandable -"

Vasigari interrupted. "The brook?"

"Yes," Marcus said. "The brook."

Vasigari smiled. "The brook gave you advice?"

"Yes."

Vasigari mulled that over for a moment.

Marcus had a thought - a brilliant thought - if *anybody* would know where to find the idol, it would be Vasigari.

"An idol," Marcus said. "*The* Idol -"

"The Idol of Trey," Vasigari said. "Yes. We've all heard of it."

Marcus said. "What I've been told... is that you have something to do with it."

She shifted her eyes aside.

"You were a good daughter," Marcus said. "... of Ebon."

Vasigari straightened up, and said, "I want you to go see the Priestess Ilia."

"That's a pseudo-random request."

Vasigari smiled. "Yes. It follows from a perfectly logical order. She happens to know where to find the *artifact*."

"Where can I find the Priestess Ilia?"

Vasigari stood still for a moment, before her eyes lit up. "Ilia exists nowhere."

"I see," Marcus said. "Then finding her may be a tad difficult."

Vasigari nodded.

"There's precisely one *pseudo-point* in common," Vasigari explained. "Zero."

Marcus lifted an eyebrow. "The number?"

"The place," Vasigari said. "Zero exists, but it also does not. Think of it as an *existence limbo*... SanCullep Island."

"SanCullep Island," Marcus said.

"You'll find her there," Vasigari said. She flashed a quick smile. "SanCullep Island doesn't exist."

Marcus exclaimed, "How do I find an island that doesn't exist?"

"Just head due south through the Sea of Tumultuous Turmoil," Vasigari explained. She smiled again. "Can't miss it." She nodded and began to walk away.

"Oh!" Vasigari exclaimed. She quickly turned around. "Before you go, I *should* warn you there is a teensy-tiny technical issue."

Marcus sighed. "Isn't there always?"

"The idol," Vasigari said, "doesn't exist."

Marcus's face dropped.   Vasigari smiled reassuringly. "Don't worry. All you need to do is prove it exists. Then you can find it."

21.   Their Eyes Shaded

For brief moments at a time, the world seemed to disappear.

Or, most likely, on the drive *to* North Carolina, I just hadn't noticed how sparsely populated the landscape was. Whenever I felt the last bit of the world may have passed by, along came another gas station or travel post.

Sheridan had a way of getting me to think great things about insignificant matters: clouds, mountains, stars. I couldn't fathom what drew my curiosity to him. Since I'd first seen him on the side of the road, I'd wondered who he was and why he was there.

Perhaps the sole purpose for his existence was to tell me a story.

He sat there, grinning as he watched the landscape roll by. "After discussing the idol with Vasigari, Marcus had a renewed sense of hope..."

- 24 -

Marcus stood in the inn lobby, contemplating the wiggling of his faint reflection in the polished wall.

Marcus smirked and exclaimed, "Hey, you!"

"Hi!" Marcus heard from behind.

Marcus jumped. Behind him stood a priestess and her two accompanying priests. The priestess grinned. "Are you

Marcus?"

Marcus slowly nodded. "Perhaps..."

"We've been looking for you," the priestess said. Her two partners nodded in unison. "Vasigari sent -"

Utica came flying down the stairs into the lobby, laughing, and holding a pile of cloth. Aspen yelled from the upper floor, "Give me back my clothes!"

Utica stopped suddenly as she bumped into the priests. The priestess snickered. She turned back to Marcus and introduced herself as Juna. Her two accomplices, Tanonoi and Ciscaforn, bowed slightly.

Juna said, "Vasigari explained you were looking for the idol. And asked us to help send you to SanCullep to find it."

"SanCullep Island is a point," Ciscaforn explained. "Which is why it doesn't exist."

"A point...," Marcus said.

"A point," Ciscaforn repeated. "The world around us has measures." He waved his hand horizontally. "It has length." He waved his hand vertically. "It has height." He waved his hand closer and away from Marcus. "It has depth. SanCullep has none of these things."

"It's a little cramped," Juna said.

"The No-People are *very* bitter about it," Tanonoi said.

Marcus nodded. He lifted an eyebrow. "*No* people?"

"It's all, perhaps, the temple's fault," Ciscaforn said. "The No-People are a bit strange. They walk with their eyes shaded and their ears plugged. I wouldn't venture near them."

Marcus scratched his head. "But if there is no dimension, how could I not?"

Juna nodded. "And that is precisely what you need to remember. If you get lost... SanCullep is but a single point. If you are in SanCullep, then you are everywhere in San-Cullep." Marcus smiled. Juna held up her finger. "But we must warn you -"

"About the -" Ciscaform said.

Tanonoi nodded. "The Temple of the Night Song."

Marcus eyed the two priests quizzically. Juna nodded. "It's a cult. They've spread over the island," she said. "Like fire, left unattended to burn in the camp."

Marcus lifted his eyebrow.

Juna said, "You'll probably have to ask Ilia for the whole story. Vasigari doesn't like to talk about it."

"They wrapped their doctrine around the Island" Tanonoi said. "We worry, and so do Ilia and Vasigari, should the cult extend beyond SanCullep, that they will wrap our towns with it too."

"Silencing those who dare to criticize them," Juna said.

"I see," Marcus said. "And I take it I am to prove they don't exist?"

"Once you leave SanCullep," Juna said, "you must prove it does not exist... or else the cult may break free." She smiled. "We trust you can succeed. You look like you've got a good grip on things."

It was at this moment that Aspen, most unfortunately, chose to burst forth from the upper floor hallway. He stood at the top of the stairs, baring all. He folded his arms, glared at Utica, and bellowed, "Utica! I insist you return my clothes!"

The priestess and the priests promptly faced away. Utica stood in silence.

"Aspen..." Marcus said, trailing a bit and carefully contemplating what to say.

"Come," Juna said. She smiled slyly. "If we do not see it, it cannot see us."

Aspen, having missed out on the entire conversation, was quite annoyed by their response. "Then who speaks? For if I am nothing, then one must wonder why you talk to yourselves."

"It is the sky," Ciscaforn said. "Perhaps we've learned

why the sky is blue."

"A cold sky," Juna said. She snickered. "A cold, cloudless sky."

The band of priests slid out the door, laughing amongst themselves. Aspen huffed, "What did they want?"

"Never mind that. We'll fill you in," Marcus said. He stared at Utica. "What were you two doing?"

Utica whistled, feigning innocence. "He was taking a nap... I did what any loving wife would do."

"I'll get you back!" Aspen exclaimed from the stairs. "Just you wait!"

Utica laughed.

"Revenge!" Aspen exclaimed. "It will be a very tasty dish!"

Elm burst through the inn office door, stopping abruptly. He gazed toward the top of the stairwell for a moment, turned around, and marched back out.

- 25 -

Adventure fever had gripped Utica and Aspen. When they told Marcus, he wondered why - not that he would mind the company.

Utica said. "We've been here for so long. I don't want to die without having lived."

Marcus smiled. "Besides," Aspen said. "I am well versed in *The Philosophy*. And I happen to think it may help us prove SanCullep exists."

Utica rolled her eyes.

As Utica and Aspen began to bicker about what provisions to bring, a floating leaf caught Marcus's eye. It twirled in the wind, bobbing up and down. It flew in little loops - growing in size with each iteration. For a moment, he could tell *exactly* where it would float next. Indeed, as he traced its path, he noticed he was tracing the path the leaf *would* follow - not that it *had* followed.

As Utica and Aspen made their plans, Marcus ran out the door to follow the leaf.

- 26 -

The leaf bobbed up and down in the wind. It sailed around trunks, branches, rocks. Marcus chased it, desperately trying to decode its pattern. To the casual observer, the leaf floated randomly, chaotically. But Marcus knew its path was *pseudo-random*. It followed from a perfectly logical order. For a brief moment, he had tuned into it.

He recalled earlier occurrences - the sunlight, water droplets, and other entities of nature in which, for even a moment, he saw clarity. *Why* was he observing these things? Perhaps this leaf held a clue, a hint, *something* that would unlock the secret.

Marcus followed the leaf to the edge of the road, where it met the water. There, the leaf landed on a rock and refused to move any further. He stared at it, waiting for it to spring back to life. The wind had died down. He sighed. He picked it up and watched it fall lifelessly into the water.

"Pardon," the brook said. "Do you mind?"

"Oh... sorry," Marcus said. He reached into the water and removed the leaf.

"Thank you," the brook said.

"Of course."

"Since the weather turned cooler... I've been fishing those things out all day," the brook said.

Marcus smiled. "I can imagine." He stared blankly at the water.

"You seem a bit... off," the brook said. "Not yourself. Quiet."

Marcus told the brook about all the times he seemed to be in tune with nature's patterns. When he finished explaining, the brook said, "Odd."

"Odd!" Marcus exclaimed. "All that... and all you have to say is odd!"

The brook laughed. "Did you expect me to say more? It's odd!"

"I *am* talking to a brook..." he shook his head.

"I can't tell you what you're seeing..." the brook said. "What you're experiencing... What you're following. But some idea, some knowledge might unlock the secret behind what you're seeing."

Marcus stared at the leaf in his hand, examining both sides. He let it drop to the ground and carefully observed its motions. "It's frustrating. I know I've found something special, but I lose it so quickly."

"You will learn in time," the brook said. "You don't need all the answers now. Nobody needs all the answers now. Wisdom takes time to gain."

"Perhaps the idol will tell me," Marcus said.

The brook just laughed. "You think the idol will give you all the answers?"

"Well... yes?" Marcus said.

"What about the journey?" the brook asked. "Wisdom follows experience."

"It's..." Marcus paused. "A *shortcut*." He smiled.

22. In Some Other Place

I could see a break in the clouds as we continued to ascend into their home. There were no stars visible through it. Of course, that didn't make sense. I shrugged it off and watched the road.

Another billboard came and went. It lurched over a steep drop far enough for drivers coming around the curve to see it. I had no clue if the numbers fell into the sequence. And really, I didn't want to know. If it weren't for the fact he kept me awake, I would have preferred to leave Sheridan by the roadside.

He chuckled to himself. "Let me tell you about the great voyage!" he exclaimed.

I glanced in the rearview mirror. Fog swirled around the road. I thought nothing of it at first. Then I noticed the billboard was gone. The outcrop it had been on now pointed the other direction...

Sheridan nodded to himself. "Most amusing tale, indeed! Utica and Aspen told Elm he spent entirely too much time at the inn, and begged him to come with them..."

- 27 -

When Marcus had been on the mainland, all he could think about was his upcoming voyage. Now that he stood on the

113

boat, watching waves crash under the stern, he could only think of home.

He overheard Utica and Aspen bickering, debating the existence of SanCullep Island. At least, that was the explanation they gave. "We were merely trying to establish its existence by means of a vote."

Marcus said, "I don't think that's how it works. Mathematics isn't a democracy."

"It's not?" Aspen asked. He curled his eyebrow and stared into space for a moment. "What is it, then? An empire? Who's the emperor?"

"*The Referee*," Marcus said. "That is what Cisero, the games-administrator, told me."

Aspen folded his arms and glared at Marcus. "Nobody sours a good bout of existence like a mathematician."

Aspen threw his arms in the air and walked away. Utica followed him, laughing. Marcus chuckled to himself and faced the sea. He wondered what the brook would think of all this. He wondered what it would say about the fish. He'd assumed fish were like people in that they moved about on their own. Yet, they came in a particular pattern. For a brief moment, he saw it. He held it. He was no longer observing how the fish moved - he knew how they would move before they did.

The water no longer glistened. Marcus scratched his head and looked up. Dark clouds rolled into view, slowly covering the sun until the sky was black and gray.

As the waves began to intensify, Elm called out from inside. "Storm! Storm approaching!"

Marcus exclaimed, "It's a storm! Man can't create this and the world is showing off its brilliance!"

Wave after wave lifted the ship and let it crash back down. Elm called again, "Come here! You'll be killed up there!"

For the first time, Marcus thought of the world and nature as something mysterious and magical. "I have a grip on things!" he exclaimed. He held tight to the railing.

With a groan and crackle of splintering wood, the boat lurched upward and crashed back to the water. A terrible screeching sounded as the iron of the boat strained. Marcus could hear Utica and Aspen scream as the boat slammed back into the waves.

"What's going on?" Elm yelled from inside.

Marcus, still holding onto the rail as tightly as possible, shouted, "I don't know! But..."

He was interrupted by a second screech. The boat rattled violently.

"Are we sinking?" Utica shouted.

"I don't know!" Marcus answered. He tried to survey the boat's condition from his station. He thought he saw a large, gray mass, with a slight hump in the center, rise out of the water. Then it dove back under.

"What *was that*?" Utica exclaimed.

Elm came running outside as the boat shuddered and flew into the air. Marcus reached out and pulled him to the rail as the boat crashed back into the water. "What are you doing?" Marcus shouted.

"We need to secure the sails," Elm said. "Or the force of the wind will tear us apart!"

The terrible sound of splintering wood sounded again as the right side of the boat tipped out of the water. Marcus held tightly onto the rail as the boat flipped on its side. He could hear a thud as Utica and Aspen fell onto the wall.

With the boat on its side, Marcus dangled from the rail. He fought to hold onto it against the heavy wind, but the rain made his hands slick. The wind caught a tilted sail and gave the left side of the boat just enough lift that it slowly righted itself.

As the boat steadied, Marcus ran as fast as he could into

the quarters. Aspen ran to the door and shut it tightly while Marcus worked to catch his breath.

"Wait," Marcus gasped.

"Elm!" Aspen exclaimed, re-opening the door.

Aspen peeked outside, but could not spot Elm through the pouring rain.

"Is he out there?" Utica asked.

Marcus froze. He wondered if Elm had lost his grip and fallen into the water.

The violent storm began to part ways with the boat. Marcus wondered if it had taken Elm with it. They all waited for a bit, not saying anything.

Convinced the worst of storm was no longer in the vicinity, Marcus crept to the door and onto the deck. He looked around. Elm was not on the boat.

"He's not out there, is he?" Utica asked.

Marcus walked back inside and shut the door. He shook his head.

Utica stared at the open sea. She watched a large shadow cast itself over the ship. The massive wave rose against the remains of the sunlight. It lifted the boat into its mouth and swallowed it whole.

- 28 -

Peoria walked alone at dusk. She did not see the brilliant sunset, the golden sky and magenta clouds. She did not see the emerging stars which lit the top of the sky. As she walked, she watched her feet. She stared at the road underneath them.

She sighed. "Highway... why didn't I tell him?"

She received no reply.

"But... he has to know, right?" she asked.

No reply.

Peoria kicked a pebble off to the side. "What if I never see him again?"

Nothing.

She asked, "And if I do... how can I let him give up the idol for me?"

A cool, quiet breeze drifted over the road.

Peoria sighed again. "I wish you would talk to me."

Peoria walked the rest of the way to the house in silence. A single leaf floated in her wake, bouncing and bobbing in wild, pseudo-random arches.

23. Lacking Perception of Anything

Just as Sheridan finished, a loud *pop* on the windshield startled me. It had started to rain. The drops, though, were unusually big.

We drove in silence for a few minutes. I watched the water streaks drift outward. My eyes were starting to dry out. I closed them for a second, then re-opened them. I found myself staring at a soft, pale face.

I jolted against the seat back. It stared at me. I swear I saw it blink before the wipers cleared the face away.

I shook my head. Sheridan was staring at me quizzically. After a moment, I simply said, "Nothing."

Sheridan nodded solemnly. I could see him grinning.

I shook my head, taking my eye off the road for a second. The windshield exploded with a sharp crack. I swerved violently as blood slipped around the glass. Sheridan sat perfectly still. I saw him out of the corner of my eye.

I slammed on the brakes. The smoke of burning rubber poured out the back of the car. When we came to a stop, Sheridan started chuckling. After convincing myself I was alive, I turned to glare at him.

"You do have to appreciate the odds," Sheridan said.

I faced the windshield again. It hadn't exploded like I first thought. A large crack extended from the upper left nearly to the lower right - clear across the diagonal. Dozens of tiny feathers were plastered to the windshield. Sheridan said, "You hit a bird."

"A *bird*!?!" I asked.

I looked again. Indeed, I had hit a bird. I noticed then how low the clouds were hanging. One of the tentacles suddenly flashed before me - almost touching the road. I jumped in my seat.

Sheridan frowned. "Poor little guy."

"You seem pretty entertained." I glared at him.

Sheridan tried to hide a smile. "Oh! It's just been one of those days."

Tell me about it, I thought. I didn't say anything, but Sheridan probably knew I was thinking it. Picking up hitchhikers! What had I been thinking? Sheridan looked my way and smiled that usual, stupid, odd smile as I pulled back onto the freeway.

- 29 -

Marcus lay on the ground in the dark, eyes closed. His head throbbed. He wanted nothing more than to fall back asleep, but he recalled the events of the past night. *Utica! Aspen!* he thought. He opened his eyes.

Nothing.

He was entirely surrounded by darkness. He closed his eyes and re-opened them, just to make sure. He could not see a thing. His pulse quickened. "Am I blind?" he asked himself.

He wondered if this is what death was - surrounded by nothing and lacking perception of anything. A low, deep crash shook the ground. Startled, Marcus sat up and slammed his head into an invisible force. He screamed as debris fell around, pushing him back down.

He opened his eyes again. A sliver of light shone above. He could hear the faint roar of the ocean. He was underneath the capsized boat, nearly crushed between the sand, the side railing, and a slab of deck. He stuck his hand through the hole, tearing down bits of the wall above until he managed to make a large enough hole to escape.

He did not know where he was. The land around him seemed strange in subtle, but noticeable ways. The roar of the ocean was a faint whisper despite his proximity to it. Birds circling above said little as they dove for food.

Marcus yelled, "Hello!" His voice carried itself nowhere and everywhere simultaneously, mixing into the background.

He did not see Utica and Aspen anywhere. Then he noticed four long streaks in the sand - presumably where two people had been dragged. The streaks extended across the beach and into the forest. Surrounding the tracks was a mess of deep footprints. Marcus feared the second-worst. What fate had befallen his friends? Perhaps he'd been spared by the boat, hidden in the cavity...

Marcus looked up toward the tree-line. There was a single gap permitting entrance into the wood. Blocking the gap stood two men, one tall and lean, the other short and stout, both well-armed and neither breathing so much as a whisper acknowledging Marcus's presence. *Maybe they are LuLinty and Kran*, he thought. *Maybe this is SanCullep Island.*

Marcus approached the men. He was not quite sure what to say to them. He waved "Hello" as he attempted to simply walk by, but stopped himself just before he walked straight into the tall man. He stepped back. "Pardon me, good gentlemen," he said. The men did not speak. They did not twitch a muscle.

"Please?" he asked.

No reply.

Marcus stood up straight, looked the tall man square in the eye and - in a stroke of bravery - demanded, "I *require* that you move at once!"

No reply.

The obvious solution - to prove they were negligible, thereby permitting Marcus to slip by - failed. Marcus realized that the island must be above such trickery.

Marcus stared at the men. They stared back in his direction, but not at him. He recalled the explanation provided by the priests. SanCullep Island did not exist. Hence, it had no length, width, or height.

Marcus turned his head toward the sky as he thought. He knew that if SanCullep was a single point, and he was *in* SanCullep, then he was *everywhere* in SanCullep, and there was only one place to be - amongst the trees.

He looked back down and no longer saw the men. In fact, the entire ocean had disappeared! He was surrounded by the forest. He stopped at an apple tree, plucked a fruit, cleaned it on his tunic, and set off down the woodlands trail.

- 30 -

Marcus passed a squirrel. He stopped for a moment to appreciate it. It had small black, beady eyes, and a bushy tail. The squirrel stood still, carefully watching him. Marcus smiled and said, "Hi, squirrel! How are you?"

The squirrel ignored Marcus.

After a moment of quiet, Marcus waved goodbye. He whistled as he walked among the trees. The sun shone brightly through the canopy, and a cool breeze gusted down the trail. Marcus thought, *I shall very much enjoy this walk. This place is not so bad.*

He then passed a squirrel. He smiled and cheerfully said, "Hi, squirrel! How are you?"

This squirrel also ignored Marcus.

Marcus whistled for a moment, then gave up. "Well... goodbye, Mr. Squirrel!"

Marcus wondered just how far the road would take him. All he knew was that he had to find Ilia and that he did not know where to find her temple. He stopped to think for a moment. He saw a brown splotch out of the corner of his eye. It was a squirrel. He said, "You sure do look familiar."

The squirrel, like the two before, ignored Marcus.

"Are you the same squirrel I saw before?" Marcus asked.

The squirrel picked up a nut. It stood still, holding its nut, staring at Marcus. Marcus scratched his head, shrugged, and bid farewell.

As he walked, Marcus took careful note of the scenery. Indeed, much of it looked familiar. Of course, the surroundings were all leaves and shrubs. It seemed odd there were no other landmarks. Marcus froze. By the side of the road sat a squirrel, holding a small nut.

Marcus folded his arms in front of his chest and stared at the squirrel. "Now, are you a *new* squirrel, or are you playing tricks on me?"

The squirrel ignored Marcus.

"Because if you are playing tricks," Marcus said, "Then I should warn you, I have a few of my own -"

The squirrel threw its nut at Marcus and scurried off. From behind him, he heard someone - a man - cracking up. "Who are you laughing at?" Marcus demanded.

The man emerged. He chuckled again and said, "You."

Marcus glared. The man smiled. "Name's Vontergeice," he said. "Vontergeice Orez."

"And where are you traveling to?" Marcus asked.

"I'm looking for my wife," Vontergeice said. "Veuleegari."

Marcus smiled, hopeful that, perhaps, Vontergeice would know Ilia's whereabouts. "Have you heard of the Priestess Ilia?"

Vontergeice stroked his chin, then shook his head. "Nope.

Haven't heard of her."

Marcus sighed. Vontergeice said, "But, then again, I've only been on the road for eleven years."

"Eleven *years*?!" Marcus exclaimed. "But -"

"Give or take one, I suppose," Vontergeice added.

Marcus asked, "How can the road be that long?"

Vontergeice said, "It's *infinitely* long, you see - for with every mile I put behind me, there are infinitely many left to go."

Marcus looked behind him. He wondered how one could reach the end of an infinite road. Vontergeice leaned against a tree and said, "A journey of an infinite number of miles begins with an arbitrary, finite number of steps. Once you take the first miles, you then take the next - subsequently and repeating in turn - until you've reached the end."

"What about Ilia?" Marcus asked. He bit his lip. "Where can I find her temple?"

As he thought, Vontergeice tapped his fingers against the wood. He then said, "*Technically*, I can't help you."

"Oh," Marcus said. "And why not?"

"SanCullep Island is but one point," Vontergeice explained. "So, algebraically, I can't exist."

Marcus scratched his head. "Algebraically, *you* can't exist?" He shook his head and blinked his eyes in surprise. Vontergeice was gone.

- 31 -

As he walked, Marcus plucked leaves off the shrubs. He examined each one - more out of boredom and frustration than anything else. "It just doesn't make sense," he said to himself. He shook his head, looking at the sky. "Is this a trap?" He threw his arms in the air. "What is this place? This world doesn't make sense!"

"It rarely does," the highway said.

Startled, Marcus leapt from his position on the roadside. A brief moment later, he asked, "Highway?"

"Yes," the highway replied.

"The same one I met before?"

"The one and only," the highway said. "What seems to be troubling you?"

Marcus sat down. He asked, "What is a road that has no end?"

"What is a road that has no beginning?" the highway asked, in turn. "For what would be your end, may very well be another's beginning."

Marcus looked about. He looked at the solitary route behind him. He looked at the solitary route ahead. He exclaimed, "I just want to have some decisions before me!" He then sighed. "I do apologize... I didn't mean to yell..."

Marcus squinted. Off in the distance, he noticed a dark spot in the trees. He quickly walked toward it and saw - indeed! A fork! He laughed. He looked down the alternate route. The fork branched into numerous other forks. He looked down the main route. It branched into even more forks. Marcus scratched his head, walked a few feet down one path, and saw even more forks. Indeed, where before there was a road and no forks, now lay forks with no roads.

24. You Proposed I Do Not Exist

Marcus couldn't decide which was worse, being trapped on an infinite road with no forks, or trapped in infinite forks with no roads. He spent the next several hours wandering aimlessly, cursing his decision to undertake this journey at all.

His attention was drawn to a little squirrel that seemed to be contemplating him even more than he contemplated the forest. The squirrel stared, beady eyes glistening in the streaks of light. For a moment, Marcus simply stared back, wondering if the squirrel would flee. But it did no such thing. *Curious little fellow, aren't you?* Marcus said, "How do I exit this place?"

The squirrel continued to stare in silence. It did not move a muscle. Marcus began to wonder if squirrels blinked their eyes, but he promptly scolded himself for getting his mind off track. "Do you not have a response for me?" he asked.

For a moment longer, it continued its blank stare. Then the squirrel twitched its tail.

"What is the nature of your silence?" Marcus asked. "For you seem to want me to say something. And I do not know what it is you wish me to say."

The squirrel continued to stare. When Marcus stepped

closer, it simply arched its head a bit higher, so that it could look Marcus in the eye. Marcus folded his arms and scolded the squirrel. "I must say, I find it quite rude that you do not respond when I speak. It's good manners to respond to someone who asks you a question! There is no need to go about mocking me for asking you."

The squirrel, still, just stared at Marcus. It twitched its tail once more, turned around, and slowly waddled off to a nearby tree. By this tree, the squirrel had a small stockpile of nuts. It ravenously dove into its little pile, eating as though there were no tomorrow. Marcus exclaimed, "Some help you are! Squirrel! Mocking me! I hope you choke!"

Marcus huffed off, marching down the twisty paths. He yelled at the trees, "Oh... I see! You, forest paths, are playing tricks on me. Well... I know what to do."

Marcus then shouted, "You don't exist!"

A little man, sitting on a tree stump, replied, "If that is the case, then why did I just startle you?"

Marcus screamed and jumped. Collecting himself, he turned around and stared down at the little man. He folded his arms and sternly replied, "That was not nice in the least! Why did you do that?"

"I asked you the very same question," the man said. "Can you not answer it?"

Marcus thought for a moment. "Well... perhaps you are just a little twert!"

"Twert? Is that a word?" the man asked.

"Twit... twerp?" Marcus said.

The man chuckled. "No... I like *twert*. And maybe I am. But I can't say you are so innocent yourself, as you proposed I do not exist!"

"Oh no!" Marcus exclaimed. "I wasn't talking to you... I just didn't see you."

The man chuckled again. "And yet you claim the forest

paths do not exist... because you cannot see them!"

Marcus stroked his chin as he thought about the situation. He grew a bit concerned. "So... you suggest there *are* forest paths? "

"I should hope not. If that is the case, you may be here a while!" the man exclaimed.

Marcus wasn't sure how the *presence* of paths could hinder his progress, but the little man, like the forest, had a way of twisting his thoughts around. "Who are you?!" he asked. "You certainly claim to know quite a bit about me!"

"As you claim of me."

Marcus threw his arms in the air and exclaimed, "I know nothing of you!"

The man shook his head. "Claiming to know nothing is far more than claiming to know what is actually false. So I must say I am sufficiently put off by your lack of modesty!"

The man folded his arms, turned away, and snuffed his nose in the air.

"Well, I have no use for one such as you," Marcus said. He faced away and snuffed *his* nose in the air.

When he heard no reply, Marcus turned back to find the man had disappeared. He stared at the empty stump for a moment, grumbled and walked off.

- 33 -

Marcus chose paths at random. None led to the exit. Every path appeared identical to the previous.

Marcus paused, and studied his surroundings *very* closely. This path, he noted, held six yellow flowers and seven blue flowers. He turned the corner, and found five yellow flowers and eight blue. He scratched his head, and examined the two options that branched from his current position.

To the left, he saw four yellow flowers and nine blue ones. To the right, he saw eight red flowers and three purple. His eyes lit up. He ran to the left. Down a branch from there, he saw, to the right, three yellow flowers and ten blue.

"I've got it!" Marcus exclaimed, following the yellow and blue flowers. He ran down subsequent paths, watching closely the declining number of yellow flowers. He stopped when he saw precisely one yellow flower. Twelve blue flowers grew nearby. He chuckled to himself. Two paths branched off. To the left, he saw three green flowers. He nodded to himself. The other path must be the correct one. He walked boldly down the right. He then looked around. Yet more paths branched off. Nearby, he saw twenty-seven black flowers and one-hundred ninety-nine opal flowers.

Marcus clenched his fists and kicked one of the opal flowers. "Oh, damn it all!" he exclaimed. Opal petals scattered all over. "Is there no end to this madness?"

Marcus turned around and found himself staring face-to-face with the same little man who'd sat on the tree stump.

"Hello!" the man said. He leaned very close to Marcus. He studied the nooks and crannies of his face as though he were the most curious and fascinating creature he'd ever seen.

Marcus let out a yelp and jumped. "Stop that!" he exclaimed. "Why do you follow me!?"

"I was not doing any such thing," the man said. "I just happened to be walking by and thought I would be friendly. You really should work on your manners."

"What's your name, anyway?"

"Name's Warren, my friend," the man said. He tipped the hat he did not wear. "And yes, I know who *you* are."

"Seems everyone here does."

Warren nodded. "Does it strike you as odd?"

Marcus folded his arms in front of his chest. He glared at

Warren. "And may I ask what you find so fascinating about me? I'm just a wanderer."

"Wonderer," Warren corrected him.

"That's what I said!"

Warren shook his head. "No. You said *wanderer*. I said *wonderer*. They sound the same, but look different." Marcus sighed. Warren continued, "One does not *wander* through a forest. They *wonder*."

"But in the forest, I wander!"

"You wander?" Warren asked. "I wonder."

Marcus *wondered* if he could be so frustrated as to pull out his hair. Warren said, "But, perhaps, it is a forest of thought. A tree of decisions."

Marcus scratched his head. Warren nodded. "The routes in life are as the paths in the woods. Where you *wonder* will take you to the next decision. So on. And so forth."

"Okay..." Marcus said. He held up his fingers, close together. "There is, perhaps, a weensy chance that your words are helpful -" Warren smiled. Marcus continued, "But how do I know the best path in life?"

Warren began to *wonder* off. As he walked away, he turned his head for a moment and said, "Follow Dots."

Marcus lifted an eyebrow. "Who?"

Warren yelled from afar, "The squirrel." He then disappeared.

"Wait!" Marcus exclaimed. "*The* squirrel!?" He sighed as he looked around. "I see no squirrel."

Marcus *wondered* about the trees, looking for Dots. He fumed about his newfound position. "A squirrel! What if Odysseus had heeded the call of a stupid *squirrel*! He wouldn't have found Penelope, that's for sure! He'd be with the sirens... eating beautiful acorns for all eternity."

And soon Marcus realized he was surrounded - not by trees - but by No-Trees. He paused a moment to clear his eyes. He looked behind him. Trees. He looked in front of him. *No*-Trees! He saw mountains in the far distance. Immediately before him was a small staircase carved in the hillside. It wound far down. A small road led the rest of the way across the valley floor. A short plateau rose slightly above the valley floor. Rising from the plateau was a peculiar structure of cyan stone, consisting of three obelisks. Perhaps... was it so?

It had to be. He laughed. At the very least, he was no longer in the maze. "Nuts to you, squirrel!" he exclaimed. "I can do this on my *own*!"

Marcus looked down. Dots stood before him, looking up, and laughing. Marcus then realized he'd only exited while looking for Dots. The squirrel laughed again. Marcus shook his fist at him as he scurried off. "You think you're so clever!" he exclaimed. "Well... I can do just fine without you!"

Ilia's temple glistened in the remains of the day's sunlight.

25. Like an Unattended Fire

- 34 -

Marcus eagerly jumped down the staircase and ran up to the temple. He stopped at the front of the building, and scratched his head. At least, he thought this was the front. But he saw no entrance. The back only had a twelve foot gap between the wall and a cliff.

Marcus circled the entire temple about twenty times, carefully running his hand along the walls. *Perhaps I'm not thinking this through,* he thought. *If SanCullep is a single point, and I am in SanCullep, then I am everywhere in SanCullep. Which means, I'm inside the temple!*

Marcus looked all around. He stared at the sky. He huffed, and decided *nothing* in SanCullep worked the way it should. *Can something exist in nothing?* he thought. He tapped on the wall. It *appeared* to be there. But as he was not inside, the temple must not be on the island.

Marcus began to walk some more, and ran straight into a rather annoyed woman. She crossed her arms across her chest and glared at him. She was fairly tall, with dark, long, curly hair. When Marcus regained his composure, she glared further. "Sir," she said. "Who are you to foul my nice clean walls?"

Marcus coughed. "Erm. I'm Marcus -"

She looked at her wall and shook her head. "Look! You got hand-prints all over it."

"I'm terribly sorry," Marcus said. "I was simply looking for the door."

The woman pointed behind her. "There it is."

Marcus looked past her. Indeed, there stood a doorway - quite large enough for four or five people to enter side-by-side. He scratched his head.

"How could you miss it?" the woman asked.

Marcus stared blankly at the woman. He then noticed the entire bottom of the temple was lined with doorways. He could see underneath and through the structure to the other side. He folded his arms and returned the woman's glare. "You're mocking me, aren't you?" he asked.

The woman smiled. "Follow me," she said. She disappeared into the temple. Despite the fact he could see through the bottom of the structure to the other end, he could not see the woman. He scratched his head again, took a deep breath, and stepped inside.

- 35 -

The woman introduced herself as Ilia. "I'm surprised you came all this way to find me," she said.

Marcus explained, "Well, Vasigari sent me -"

Ilia interrupted. "I meant, through the confusion of trees and such. It seems silly."

"Silly..." Marcus repeated.

Ilia nodded. "Of all people, I would have assumed you'd have figured it out. SanCullep is a point, and so, if the door connects to a place *on* SanCullep, it connects to *every* place on SanCullep."

Marcus slapped his forehead with his palm. "You can see," Ilia explained, "why I have to make that door rather elusive... otherwise, I have all sorts of folks poking their heads into my temple - and as you may have learned, the island is not exactly a friendly place."

Marcus looked back toward the entry. "I've seen," he muttered.

Ilia said, "Take a seat."

Marcus looked around for a chair. The room was entirely void of any furniture at all. He looked up at Ilia, who stared back impatiently. "It makes me nervous if you're standing the whole time," she said. She sat down.

Marcus scratched his head. Ilia asked, "What's wrong?"

"What do I sit on?" Marcus asked. He tried to figure out what Ilia, herself, sat upon.

"The chairs don't exist. Just take one."

Marcus shrugged and pulled up a non-existent chair. Ilia nodded.

"Perhaps I should tell you the rest of the story... after where your friend Aspen left off."

Marcus lifted an eyebrow. "How do you know where he left off?"

Ilia lifted her finger. "Vasigari told me." She smiled. "I remember like it was yesterday...

"I wanted to be an engineer. I wanted to build great structures. Vasigari was my friend because she liked to imagine what it would be like to live in my cities. We would spend all day in the fields, dreaming of what all we would build there.

"There was a peculiarity to the field that I still can't quite describe. It was our field. A piece of cloth tied to a stick was our flag. When we planted it, it became the flag of a great nation. The pile of rocks we made became a tower. The pond we built by making a little dam became our expansive sea. We learned out there that reality is as we defined it. We had a power we did not know how to wield."

Marcus's eyes lit up. "Like Fred!"

"Fred?" Ilia raised an eyebrow.

"A dream... I think. One day I lost track of my own existence," Marcus said. "Master Sophus said I'd make a fine mathematician one day."

Ilia smiled. "*My* dreams were not proper for a young woman. The thought didn't even cross the elders' minds that we would be doing something other than sneaking out to meet some lover. After all, our friends were up to *other* sorts of mischief. The council decided to not allow youth to stray far from the town.

"So, Vasigari and I came up with a scheme. We made up the Giant Dachy. Whenever the council elders asked why we strayed so far, we told them we were chased. I suppose I should have been more worried about what would happen if they *did* believe us, rather than if they did not. They locked the entire village down. It was really quite remarkable how many idiots governed that place."

Marcus snickered. "I wouldn't know anything about that."

"I'm *sure* things have changed since my time."

"Well, the Dachy has been defeated, now."

Ilia grinned. "Eight of us - Vasigari, myself, and six of our friends, decided we had enough. I came up with the Temple of the Night Song. The monks of the temple had sent for us. The monks had heard of our peril, and claimed to have a remedy. All of us approached the hall, but I was the one who spoke with the governor first."

Ilia grabbed Marcus's face. "He held my cheeks in his hands when he spoke, as if I were really going to face away. 'Ilia! My dear! It is much too dangerous. We will send ourselves to meet your monks.' "

She then let go of his face. " 'No!' I exclaimed. 'The monks sent for *us*. It is the only way.'

" 'Well,' someone else interrupted." Ilia stared into space as she thought. "I think his name was Victor. Or, Vector.

'They need youthful bodies...' He had to stop to think.

"And that's when I came up with *it* - 'To build the idol,' I said. 'An idol - *The* idol - which grants wisdom.'

"Victor came up with the next part. 'Yes. Wisdom to know how to defeat the Giant Dachy.'

" 'The... idol?' the elder asked."

Marcus said, "The idol that grants infinite wisdom!"

Ilia nodded. She grinned. "I came up with that part.

" 'The Idol of Trey.' I pointed to the stars. 'An idol which grants its bearer infinite wisdom. Wisdom for free, without needing to live the life to obtain it.'

" '*Trey*?' the elder asked.

" I asked him, 'See the North Star?'

"The elder nodded.

" 'Look just to the right. There is a line of four stars that form an arch. Then there are two stars just below the arch. One to the left of the middle and one to the right... and to the right of the arch are three stars that form a small triangle.'

" 'That's Trey?' he asked.

" 'A flying dog who watches over the interests of those curious about the world and nature,' I said. 'The monks are old. And feeble. They cannot complete the task.' "

Marcus looked out the window. He imagined that with a sky full of stars, one could visualize just about anything.

Ilia continued, " 'Only the young can build such an idol,' one of the other young men said. I think he went by Roz.

" 'I don't understand,' the elder pleaded.

"I didn't understand, either. Neither did Roz. Since he was stuck for ideas, I came up with yet another. 'Why would a wise man such as yourself need the idol when you have so much wisdom already?' I said. 'It takes... an *empty vessel* to sail the great sea of tumultuous turmoil.' "

Marcus asked, "So, that's your sea?"

"Of course!" Ilia replied. "Then the councilman sighed.

He looked toward the horizon and bit his lip. 'If it is the only way.'

" 'Send us out again,' Victor said. The other sons and daughters nodded. 'We will brave the cold world.'

" 'But you're our good sons and daughters!' the elder exclaimed. 'We are here to protect you!'

" 'It is our turn to be heroes of Ebon,' Vasigari said.

" 'To be so honorable,' the councilman said. He wiped a tear from his eye. 'We'll send you with all you need to bring peace to the rest of Ebon's good sons and daughters.'

"Victor smiled. 'We will build the Idol of Trey. We will return with infinite wisdom. We will visit the Temple of the Night Song and they will rid us of this horrible plague.'

"Perhaps they saw it as a rite of passage. I'll never know. We never returned."

Marcus briefly stared at Ilia, unsure of what to say.

"It's not an easy state of affairs," Ilia said. "To be told you can't do what you wish..."

"I can imagine," Marcus said.

"I got to build my city after all... complete with its inhabitants. And then we forgot about it!" Ilia said. "We had our fun and left. And the temple spread. Wildly. Like an unattended fire, it grew out of our control."

"So, they're here," Marcus said. "I don't understand. Why the concern?"

"We think one of the temple's members escaped," Ilia said.

Marcus gazed out the window.

Ilia explained, "He... or she, whichever the case may be, is crafty. Crafty enough to shift out of non-existence. And if that person comes to understand existence, they could prove SanCullep exists and allow the rest to escape."

"Mathematics is not for the faint of heart," Marcus said.

Ilia nodded. "When you leave, you must be sure to prove that SanCullep *does not* exist."

Marcus tilted his head. "I thought that was already done?"

Ilia shook her head. "No. Neither case is proven. Call it existence limbo."

Marcus stared at his hands.

"Yes," Ilia said. "It will be difficult, I'm sure... but I must admit I do not know the inner-workings of non-existence proofs. All I know is that if SanCullep exists, so does the Night Song."

"Okay," Marcus said. "I guess that would explain why Vasigari wanted me to come here."

Ilia nodded. "She is convinced the only way to prove the cult, and the island, does not exist is to show the world itself does not exist."

"Ah!" Marcus exclaimed. "She never did give me a motive."

Ilia shrugged. "She's special," she said.

She stared out the window for a moment and smiled. "You can explain it to me, because I'm not good at these things. Vasigari said the existence of the idol implies the non-existence of the world."

Marcus pondered that prospect for a moment. He said, "I suppose I'd need to see the idol first."

"I see." Ilia frowned, looking toward the door. "Then, tomorrow, we should discuss the idol."

"Tomorrow."

Ilia nodded. "You're welcome to any of the beds."

"They don't exist," Marcus said.

Ilia stood up and began to walk away. "Of course they don't," she said. "But you're a mathematician. Just prove that one does."

- 36 -

Marcus spent the night in the altar room - the only room in the temple with a window. He spent most of the night staring out of it, watching the moon. The moon was comforting. It reminded him that the world outside SanCullep still existed.

He'd expected to fall asleep easily, but found he could not stop thinking of Utica and Aspen. He was not sure if he could make it home without them. Of course, at this point, he wasn't even sure he could find the coast again.

Eventually, he nodded off.

- 37 -

Ilia glared at Marcus. She reached into the shadows behind her, pulling out a figurine. Marcus's eyes grew large.

Ilia tossed the figurine to Marcus. "Catch!"

The figurine resembled a tiny dog, fashioned out of various, randomly chosen items. It had a black pearl nose, small dishes for the ears, and opal beads for the eyes. Marcus protested. "I can touch it. I can hold it. I can see it! How can you tell me this does not exist?"

Ilia said, "Reality is as you define it. Sight, sound, touch, these are all things which you perceive and interpret. Few in this world will comprehend that. Sometimes man's greatest fears are of things that do not exist. Sometimes he lets these fears consume him."

Marcus tossed the idol lightly in his hand.

"After we left Ebon, Vasigari and I split from the others. We wanted to *do* something with our freedom. Of course, the first thing we did was make up that silly cult."

Marcus nodded.

"And the idol," Ilia said. "*And* the Giant Dachy. Eventually, we decided we should clean up our mess." She paused for a moment. "As you know, non-existence proofs can be tricky. Which is why we're so impressed with *you*. See, I tried to prove the idol, the Dachy, and the cult did not exist. But in the attempt, I proved I didn't exist."

"So that's how you got here?"

"Yes," Ilia said. "And Vasigari tried to rescue me. In effect, she proved she exists everywhere."

"Everywhere but here."

"If you exist in all places," Ilia explained, "then you do not exist in a No-place."

Marcus said, "So I'm in -"

"Zero."

Marcus stared blankly toward the window. The sky, void of any weather, was still dark despite the fact it was "morning."

"*Anyway,*" Ilia said. "I know Vasigari is not the patient type, so I won't keep you any longer."

Marcus tossed the idol in his hand again. He couldn't shake the fear that he would convince himself the idol didn't exist and it would suddenly disappear.

"The door is behind you."

Indeed, there was a door. However, there was no scenery outside. Marcus tried to shrug it off. "I need to find Utica and Aspen."

"The friends you arrived with."

"Yes..." Marcus said. He eyed the door again. Only a black film was visible through its frame. He asked, "You wouldn't happen to know their whereabouts... would you?"

"No," Ilia said. "Of course, there's really only one place they could be."

Marcus took a deep breath and walked through the door. The black film swallowed him whole.

26. Chanting Existence Hypotheses

I stared... *glared* at Sheridan. He smiled innocently - as he always did when he knew I didn't quite follow.

"It's... *weird*." I wasn't quite sure how to word it. "It doesn't... make sense. Isn't this supposed to be a *history*... not a, you know, fictional story?"

Sheridan nodded slowly. I asked, "Then... how do all these weird things happen?"

Sheridan started to explain, "Who is to say they're -"

I interrupted. "Is this like... Marcus's dream? Is he mad?"

Sheridan paused for a moment. He cracked a smile. "In almost any math text you'll find the phrase, 'proof has been left as an exercise for the reader.' I say, '*The nature of reality* is an exercise for the reader,' " he said. "It means you'll learn more for having figured it out for yourself..."

- 38 -

When Marcus stepped out of the black film, he promptly walked into a tree.

Marcus groaned, took a step back, and looked about. Ilia's Temple had sat atop a distinct, short plateau on which there were, quite clearly, no trees. *No-Trees*, of the genus *Nothing*, were quite abundant in the fields of SanCullep. Their most distinctive feature was that, when run into, they did not hurt the nose. Since Marcus's nose hurt, he could *conjecture* he'd run into a tree of the "existence" family and was no longer on the plateau. Odd, because he had been *before* he entered the temple.

Ilia's plateau also held no rocks, no pits, and oddly enough, no monsters, Marcus thought. He then grew very concerned. *Since there are no No-Trees, it could very well be the case there are no No-Rocks, no No-Pits, or even worse, no No-Monsters. All the things which Ilia's plateau did not have, could now not not be.*

Before him, Marcus saw a welcome-sign, written in a pleasant font, which read "Welcome to Lenrek," underneath that, "Population: o."

Odd, Marcus thought, *the last person to leave had to care enough to alter the sign*. But the town was quite beaming with life. *These must be the No-People.*

The No-People droned about in complete and utter silence. They shuffled systematically, robotically, as if they were trains on a set track. It was only when Marcus stepped into the town square that they broke form - buzzing around him - silently at first, then noisily.

"Utica!" Marcus shouted. "Aspen!"

The townspeople did not even seem to hear. Or care. But Marcus overheard:

"You know what *The Philosophy* says about retribution?"

"Two onions in a basket make you cry twice as hard as one, if both happened to be chopped!"

"And don't forget to savor the onion milk, if onions were mammals and produced milk for consumption!" followed by mutual chuckling and nodding.

Marcus scratched his head. This must be the same *Philosophy* that Aspen was always quoting. Once he really listened to the townspeople, he heard they were all quoting it.

"But you know what *The Philosophy* says about greed - A rooster that eats its own eggs is not a rooster, because roosters don't lay eggs, hens do."

"And don't stand under the watermelon tree, if watermelons did grow on trees, because it would hurt if a watermelon fell from the branch and hit your head!"

Marcus interrupted the two. "Virtue is like a cat falling into a body of water. The cat will smell damp for the next few hours."

Two townspeople paused, staring at him in silence. Soon the other passerby began to slow down, then stop. They stared. Marcus stared back, and began to regret speaking at all. After an awkward moment, one finally said, "You're not among us... are you?"

"Perhaps not," Marcus said. "I'm a traveler... looking for -"

A third and fourth townsperson approached. One spoke up. "You must leave -"

Marcus jumped back when he saw the first townsperson slowly fade away. The second said, "Your existence implies our non-existence."

Soon two more townspeople joined. Marcus realized they were beginning to form a circle around him. He stepped back. The fifth townsperson said, "You must leave!"

Marcus contemplated how his existence implied the non-existence of the villagers. Perhaps it was due to the fact the town had No-People. Marcus's presence meant the town's population included him, and hence, no No-People. Thus, the No-People couldn't be. He saw the fear in their eyes as they began, one-by-one, to fade away. He knew well enough that fear drives the worst in men. They would remove him one way or another.

Marcus took off down the street. The townspeople followed, waving their arms and fists, chanting existence hypotheses to the contrary of their non-existence.

The streets twisted and turned in confusing and meaningless directions. North was south and west was north-east. Marcus ran east, toward the setting sun, which was also a rising sun because it lay to the north, which was west. The townspeople followed, attempting in turn to prove *Marcus* didn't exist. Marcus wondered if he was about to fade as well.

As he ran, he looked behind himself. He saw only trees. The town had disappeared.

He faced forward just as he collided with a wall. He hit his head - hard - and everything went black.

- 39 -

Marcus woke with a splitting headache. He cracked his eyes open. The sky above was slightly yellow; the sun hanging low. The trees' leaves swung lightly in the breeze. He shook his head and sat up. He wondered how long he had been knocked out. Before him stood a wall with two very distinct features. At the base sat some tiny, loose pebbles. Just above them was a head-sized dent.

To the right was a small sign. It read "Temple of The Silver Money." To the left was a large opening. A trail led through the gate to a tall, windowless building. He scratched his head. The structure was ornamented with monkey faces - one after the other in neat little lines along the edges. He looked at it again. He rubbed his eyes and read the sign correctly this time: "Temple of the Silver Monkey."

Marcus stood up and approached the temple. He was immediately stopped by the guards. One was *very* stocky. The other was *very* tall, and lean. The stocky guard, standing on the left, had a peculiar looking mustache. It resembled a monkey's rump and tail. Marcus thought it to be *peculiarly peculiar*.

The left guard introduced himself as Gonsig, and his part-
ner, Barrdy. "Who are you to approach the temple?" Barrdy
said. He waved his spear in Marcus's face.

Marcus smiled innocently. "I'm Marcus!" he exclaimed.

Barrdy's eyes lit up. He lifted an eyebrow. "Say... *The*
Marcus?"

"The one and only," Marcus said. He took a short bow.

Gonsig laughed. "And I suppose if we don't let you
through, or at least, spare your life, you will prove we don't
exist?"

"Well, I wouldn't be so bold as to propose you do not
exist," Marcus said. "Such a course of action would be rather
unfriendly! There's enough unfriendliness in nature - what
with lightning strikes and bear's teeth and what not - to go
about purposely looking for it..."

Gonsig frowned. Barrdy punched his arm. Gonsig then
stood up straight and glared at Marcus.

Marcus shook his head. "So, I wasn't saying you don't
exist! I was merely suggesting you haven't given the matter
much thought. It is important to consider these things, you
know. How can you know where you are going - or from
where you come, if you have not established that you *are* to
begin with?"

"I.... I don't know," Gonsig said. Barrdy shuddered.

"For, surely, these matters are important!" Marcus argued. "If you do not exist, you have no business floating
about the world... and certainly no business manipulating
anything in it!"

"I'd hate to get in trouble," Gonsig said.

"I'd hate for you to, as well!" Marcus exclaimed. "There
are enough ways to stumble into trouble without going about
looking for it. Do you exist? Do you not? It is a matter of
where the burden of proof lies. Does the fact you can't prove
you exist imply that you don't? Or does it imply you *do* exist,

because you can't prove that you do not?"

Gonsig blinked. "What if we can't establish our existence?" he asked. He looked down at himself. "I think I do, though."

Barrdy grew quite worried. "It's Marcus, though. He is a great hero. Why, if he says we don't exist then perhaps we really don't."

Gonsig looked around nervously. "You may be right. Otherwise, he would lack his reputation."

Marcus lifted an eyebrow. He scratched his head.

"We don't exist!" Barrdy cried. "What do we do?"

"Umm... just don't touch anything," Marcus replied. He tried to figure out just how, exactly, he'd convinced the guards they didn't exist. He shrugged.

Marcus slipped through the doorway. He turned around for a moment to watch Gonsig and Barrdy. They had completely stripped their clothing and were patting themselves down - attempting to convince themselves all their parts existed. Marcus faced away once more. "It's all about being in tune with your Non-Sense," he said to himself.

- 40 -

Marcus wandered aimlessly as he wondered about the decor. The tops of the interior walls were lined with carefully carved monkey faces. They were mostly uniform, but every now and then, one had its ear twitching or its tongue hanging out. He wondered if, perhaps, the artist had a bit of fun at someone's expense.

A loud screech - half screech, half wail, echoed down the chambers. Marcus covered his ears.

When the sound stopped, Marcus uncovered his ears and looked around. The hallway spanned infinitely in both directions. *Yet, the sound appears closer*, he thought. He wondered if sound can *appear* at all, as it's only things one can see that *appear*. If sound was sight, then sight was sound. As Marcus followed the screech, he studied the decor some more. Perhaps the faces were some sort of code. Marcus contemplated a group of faces that resembled a particular pattern. However, it made no sense. He scratched his head.

He heard his name called, "Marcus!"

Marcus's ears perked up. He looked to the left and right, but did not see any alternate doorways. The hallway spanned in only two directions - toward the screeching, and from which he came. But again, he heard his name, "Marcus! Over here!"

"Here?" Marcus asked. "Or *hear*? Because they look the same, but sound different."

"No," the voice said. "They *sound* the same, but *look* different!"

Marcus nodded, and realized sight was, indeed, sight - and sound was, indeed, sound. Sound didn't *appear*, sight *appeared*. And with the correct orientation, Marcus then saw he was facing a wall. He scratched his head, looking left and right. The hallway spanned in two directions, but perpendicular to the path he'd been on. As usual, one path led toward the screeching. The other led to a small chamber.

"Marcus!" someone exclaimed.

Marcus ran toward the chamber. Inside was a small jail. Behind the bars stood Utica and Aspen. Utica jumped excitedly. "Marcus! You're outside!"

Marcus tapped on the bars. He looked Utica and Aspen directly in the eyes. "*How* did you two end up in here?"

Utica explained, "Well, we *were* looking for you! We looked all around the boat."

"Nothing," Aspen said, "But then, we saw these tracks leading to the woods and thought maybe you'd been captured or something."

Marcus nodded. He scratched his head. "Odd, because I saw those tracks and thought *you* were captured!"

"Then!" Utica exclaimed. She glared at Aspen. Aspen smiled innocently. "Aspen punched one of the guards... Rank, or something like that."

"Kran," Marcus said.

"He wouldn't acknowledge me!" Aspen exclaimed.

"And out of the blue, we were in here!" Utica exclaimed. "I don't even remember being taken here."

Aspen nodded. "It's... odd. All of a sudden, we were here with Mr. Bones."

Marcus looked down at the floor. Aspen kicked the remains of a skeleton.

"And then there's the screeching," Utica said.

Marcus nodded. On cue, the screeching echoed down the hallway. Aspen covered his ears.

"What *is* that?" Marcus asked.

"We don't know!" Utica exclaimed.

"It must be the guards," Aspen said. "Kran. And his friend."

"Say," Utica said. "How did *you* get by them?"

"SanCullep is just a single point," Marcus explained. "So if I am *on* SanCullep, I am *everywhere* on SanCullep."

"Eh?" Aspen said. His eyes glazed over. Another screech echoed down the hall.

Marcus started to re-explain, but Utica exclaimed, "Wait!" She paused a moment to think. "I think I see. If you draw a dot on a piece of paper, and that's a map of the entire world, then once you've stepped onto that dot... you've been to all the places on it."

"Then how -" Aspen said.

Utica and Marcus both smiled. A third screech echoed, louder than before. Marcus patted Aspen on the shoulder. "Come on," he said. "Let's get out of here before we realize we're all *in* the jail."

- 41 -

Marcus stopped at a pile of papers. They lay scattered about the side of the corridor - as if someone had swept them, like leaves, into the street gutter to be carried away with the rain. Aspen was the first to notice their peculiar contents. He read one aloud, "He who has the last word is the most likely to be called an ass."

Utica rolled her eyes. Aspen read another, "Sometimes the reluctant warrior is the warrior with a bee in his armor."

"They sound like... *Philosophy* quotes," Marcus said.

Aspen ruffled through more of the papers. "They all do," he said.

"Perhaps..." Utica said. "We have found where they are written?"

"But..." Aspen said. He scratched his head. "In the temple of the Monkeys?"

"Ah!" Marcus exclaimed. His eyes grew wide and he nodded proudly. "You've always said the books seemed to pop up out of nowhere. *This* is nowhere!"

Utica smiled. "We have found the only place one could churn out so much dribble."

Aspen rolled his eyes.

Marcus led Utica and Aspen to a small door bearing a large, carved monkey face. Marcus looked back. Utica and Aspen motioned Marcus to open it. He shrugged, and slowly pulled it open.

When Marcus stepped into the chamber, the title *The Philosophy of Many Hands* immediately became clear. As soon as his eyes adjusted to the bright light, he focused on the floor of the great chamber. Before him stood hundreds upon hundreds of tiny monkeys. They jumped wildly, excitedly about the room - screeching and howling under the vast beams of light.

Upon the floor were many colored tiles; each one a unique shade. Along the edges walked a handful of scribes, carefully recording what tiles the monkeys hit.

Utica burst out laughing. "I knew it!"

Aspen folded his arms and glared at Utica. "I *still* say it's a wonderful philosophy."

"It's a *pseudo-random* number generator," Marcus said.

"And like all good random number generators," Utica said, "its philosophy makes sense only to the interpreter."

Utica picked up a scroll from a bin neatly labeled "Fresh Thoughts." She read aloud, "The cat's milk is most delightful if you milk the cat yourself; For it would have likely clawed your eyes out during the process of milking it, and your other senses would be stronger as compensation for the blindness."

"That's horrible!" Aspen exclaimed. "You can't milk a cat!"

Marcus picked up a scroll from a bin labeled "Rejects." He read aloud in a deep, clear voice, "Die, die, die."

"That doesn't sound random to me," Utica said. "It's the same thing repeated!"

Marcus shrugged. "That's the rub to randomness. You have to keep the outliers. It's bad mathematics otherwise!"

Marcus carefully set the scroll in the "Fresh Thoughts" bin. Aspen stared at the monkeys.

"I fail to see..." Utica said. She was interrupted, though, when a single little monkey waddled up to her. She smiled. "Awww... how *cute*! Aren't you just the most precious thing!" She exclaimed. She rubbed the monkey on its head.

As Utica turned to face Marcus and continue their discussion, the monkey grinned and slapped Utica on her rear. "Hey!" she shouted.

Marcus laughed.

"I've been monkey-violated!" Utica exclaimed.

The monkey grinned again. "Hey... that's my wife!" Aspen scolded.

"It's just a monkey," Marcus said. "It doesn't know!"

The monkey let out a few more squeaks that almost sounded like chuckling. It slapped Utica's rear again.

"You little scoundrel!" Aspen said. He lowered himself eye-to-eye with the monkey and glared icily at it. The monkey slapped his face.

"A wise guy!" Aspen exclaimed. He slapped the monkey.

The monkey huffed and slapped Aspen. For a few moments, the two traded slaps, until Utica protested. "I don't think you're accomplishing much..."

A second monkey joined the first, stared Aspen eye-to-eye, and slapped his face. Aspen slapped the second monkey, only to be slapped again by the first. Soon a third monkey joined in the fray, and a bit afterward, a fourth.

"Uh-oh," Marcus muttered as more monkeys approached. Some began screeching and hollering. Marcus gulped and turned toward Utica and Aspen. "Back away," he whispered.

As the three backed out the chamber door, the monkeys slowly followed. When the three sped up, the monkeys did as well. Soon Marcus, Utica, and Aspen found themselves running as fast as they could down the corridor until they reached the end. Marcus slammed the door to the chamber. He could hear the banging of a dozen monkeys crashing into it.

Utica exclaimed, "We're in the jail room!"

Marcus scratched his head. Aspen exclaimed, "Where's the exit? How did *you* get in?"

"I don't know," Marcus said. "I just walked in... and then the corridor turned perpendicular on itself."

The door cracked as one of the monkeys slammed into it. "Let's go!" Utica exclaimed.

"Where?" Aspen yelled back. He held his ears. The screeching penetrated the door and bounced along the walls. Marcus slowly approached the door. Utica eyed him.

She asked, "What are -" Marcus held up his finger.

He said quietly, "Ilia told me her door was elusive because it connected to any point on SanCullep."

Utica and Aspen stared at each other. Marcus put his hand on the door handle. Utica was about to scream for Marcus to halt, when he quickly pulled the door open. Utica and Aspen stared in disbelief at the empty chamber before them. Marcus stepped cautiously through the doorway. He laughed. "It's Ilia's temple," he said.

Utica stepped through after him. She took Aspen's hand and pulled him through. They took a moment to adjust to the quiet. They were under the temple, among the support pillars. The mountains and plateau were visible in all directions.

Utica and Aspen both remained speechless. Marcus took their hands and led them through the doorway formed between two of the pillars.

- 42 -

Marcus hit the sand first. He stumbled as his feet sank deep into the terrain. Utica and Aspen followed, and nearly collided with each other. They took a moment to catch their breath. Aspen shook his head in bewilderment. Utica stared blankly at the beach. LuLinty and Kran stood behind them, guarding the gap in the line of trees. Marcus was elated. For once, something on SanCullep worked the way he'd expected! The doorways in Ilia's temple connected to any opening on SanCullep - including the path LuLinty and Kran blocked. His relief didn't last long. Something was missing.

The tracks and footprints were gone.

Utica was the first to ask, "What happened to our boat?"

Indeed, the boat was high up the beach - nearly to the tree-line. Marcus kicked the sand around it. "The tide," he said. He sighed, and began to drag the boat toward the water. Utica and Aspen helped him. The boat was very heavy; it took them nearly twenty minutes to get it to the water's edge.

Marcus paused. He looked at the sea, then back to the boat. He recalled the storm that brought him here. He realized the boat had a mast again, and the hull repaired. He then stared at the ground.

In the sand were four very distinct tracks, carved by the boat's frame as it slid. Around the tracks was a mess of footprints. Utica tapped Marcus on the shoulder. "What are you staring at?"

"SanCullep is but a single point," Marcus said. "If I am on SanCullep, then I am everywhere on SanCullep."

Utica lifted an eyebrow. Marcus continued, "Am I *anytime* on SanCullep as well?"

"Let's *go!*" Aspen yelled. He pointed toward the horizon. Dark, ominous clouds hung low, casting a deep shadow over the water. "There's a storm approaching."

27. We Were Naive

I interrupted him. "How can you tell me a story about a place in which all time is a single point in time?"

"Well, you're making an assumption that you may not want to make."

"That it... I... okay, I don't know."

Sheridan thought quietly for a moment. "This tale has been taken from writings, copied from writings, copied from other writings which were taken from Marcus's own. Don't assume he understood the nature of SanCullep Island correctly."

I wasn't sure what to believe. Sheridan added, "But... you'll find out." He smiled. "In time, we'll see just how right or wrong he was."

- 43 -

Marcus shouted at Utica and Aspen to take cover. Massive waves crashed from above. They had been at sea for only a moment, but already the fierce current pushed SanCullep far into the distance. It was barely visible through the sheets of rain.

Marcus slid on his belly across the deck. At the front of the boat, a large sail bulged. He knew that if the mast snapped, the boat would be impossible to maneuver. He had

to roll the sail up. Utica screamed through the wind for him
to return inside.

A wave picked the boat up, tossed it into the air, and let
it drop. Marcus held onto the side rail, clinging so tightly his
fingertips began to bleed.

"Marcus!" Aspen yelled. "Look -"

Aspen's voice was drowned out by a second wave and a
long creak. Marcus looked up just before the mast struck his
head.

- 44 -

Marcus awoke on the shore. His first thought was that he
was back on SanCullep. But when he opened his eyes, the
sky appeared clear. The roar of the waves sounded clear. The
world seemed *right*. He was back on the mainland.

"You were out for quite a while," Utica said. She sat on
the sand, leaning over him.

Marcus rubbed his head. It was sore. He had a large
bump on the top, above his right eye, and a splitting headache.
He sat up and looked around the beach. Aspen was off in the
distance, tending a small fire.

"Where are we?" Marcus said.

Utica shrugged. "Aspen says we're about where we took
off from. But this doesn't look familiar."

Marcus nodded. Utica explained, "We couldn't carry you.
And neither of us felt like walking, anyway. So we camped
here last night."

"I see," Marcus said. He looked down the beach again.

He remembered waking up on SanCullep for the first
time. Every sight on SanCullep had seemed to blend into
one big mass. Looking at something had been like trying to
pick out a distant conversation in a crowded hall. It could
be done, but required almost total concentration. Now that

he was home, listening and seeing seemed much easier than before he'd left.

Utica hung her head. "Elm didn't make it," she said. She looked out toward the water. "When the boat capsized."

Marcus stared silently. He thought she already knew that. He'd been lost when the monster struck the boat before they'd landed on SanCullep. He couldn't think of an appropriate way to word the question, though. He said, "I was upset when we first found out, too."

Utica tilted her head. "How did you know?"

"How did I know?" Marcus asked.

"Yes," Utica said. "Don't you remember? He was helping you secure the sails. Then the mast snapped and hit your head. I don't know *how* he managed to get you into the cabin. Then the boat capsized."

"He was helping me..." Marcus said.

Utica nodded.

"But where was he on SanCullep Island?" Marcus asked.

"SanCullep Island..." Utica said.

"We lost him on the first leg of the journey. *Before* we landed on SanCullep."

"We never found the island," Utica said. "Which, after some rational thinking, makes sense. How could we find a non-existent island?"

"But -" Marcus said.

Tears welled up in Utica's eyes. She said, "It was fun. We don't blame you. We wanted an adventure. You provided. But..." She took a moment to look over the water. She stood up. "We were naive."

Utica then walked away. Marcus stared silently after her. She joined Aspen near the fire. He didn't have a chance to ask her if she blamed *Juna*, the priestess, and her accomplices. He wondered if, perhaps, their memory had been erased. After all, on SanCullep Island, all time was one point. So it made sense they would have zero seconds of memory. But Marcus couldn't figure out how *he* had memory of it. He shook his head. Perhaps he'd dreamt the whole thing while he was knocked out.

Utica and Aspen stood over the fire, cooking something. The smell began to waft his way. A warm meal would set things right. He climbed to his feet and started to walk along the shore. He realized just how foggy his memory of the sea journey was. He wondered what he had written in his roll of paper about it. He reached in his satchel and pulled out the Idol of Trey.

IV
The Defense of Research

28. You Will Regret It

I was having flashbacks to earlier in our trip. Each time the fog lowered, then rose, the landscape looked different than before.

It was hard to tell what was happening. It was so dark out. There was no moon, no stars, no *anything* other than the car's headlights. Perhaps the road was just playing tricks on me.

I wanted to think that. But each time I was tempted to dismiss the entire evening altogether, my attention focused on one thing. In the past hundred miles, we had not passed a single vehicle, nor had we passed any lights.

"It's like the world's disappeared," Sheridan said. He studied the empty void.

I didn't want to think about it.

- 45 -

Marcus paced up and down the stretch of highway just before the inn. He missed Peoria greatly. But, he worried about Utica and Aspen. After returning to the inn, he had hardly spoken two words to them. While not outwardly angry, he could tell they blamed him for Elm's demise. They'd said nothing when he presented the idol. Nothing!

Perhaps they were too upset to think clearly. Perhaps they

thought he built an idol himself to try to justify the trip. Perhaps...

He gave up thinking of possibilities. It was clear they were upset, and they did not believe they had been to SanCullep.

Truth be told, Marcus had a hard time believing it himself. "An island that doesn't exist!" he said, aloud, "It's silly!"

Yet, he had to believe it. After all, he had the idol. He inspected every nook and cranny of the figurine. It sparkled in the sunlight. "Something that doesn't exist wouldn't sparkle," he said.

He held the idol over the tall grass and let it drop. It made a soft *thud*. "Something that doesn't exist wouldn't make a sound," he said. He picked the idol up.

"I can tell you've had quite the adventure," Vasigari said.

Marcus jumped, turned around, and glared at her. "You like to do that, don't you?"

Vasigari smiled. "Sorry. I forgot *you* can only see what is visible before you."

Marcus stared at Vasigari. She nodded. "I was worried you may not make it back. What is it like there? How is Ilia?"

"Ilia..." Marcus said. "She is..." Vasigari stared at Marcus with wide eyes. Marcus continued, *"interesting."*

Vasigari smiled. "I thought you'd like her."

"She told me why you wanted me to get the idol," Marcus said. He stared at the figure for a moment. "She said you wanted me to get it so I could give it to you... you couldn't get it yourself because you live in mutually exclusive sets."

Vasigari shifted her eyes. Marcus continued, "It doesn't grant wisdom, does it?"

Vasigari grinned, slightly, for a moment. She then said, "Why would you think not?"

"Because Ilia said it," Marcus said. "Its very being, somehow, proves the world does not exist."

"And are you not wiser for having obtained it?"

He said, "Tell me how it proves the world does not exist."

Vasigari sighed. "It is a *proof by contradiction*. I need the idol to tell you the proof. If I had the proof now, I wouldn't need the idol." She smiled. "So... can I have it?"

Marcus looked further down the road. He glanced at the idol. If he gave it to Vasigari, he could not give it to Peoria's master. If he gave it to Peoria's master, he could not give it to Vasigari. She stared impatiently, crossed her arms, and huffed. "I'm a busy woman," she said.

Marcus slipped the idol into his satchel. He stood up, straightened his posture, and said, firmly, "No."

Vasigari stood quietly. Marcus hadn't the slightest idea what would follow. Indeed, neither did Vasigari. Marcus's response came so unexpectedly that, for the first time, her persistent slight grin disappeared. "No?" she asked.

"No."

Vasigari stared blankly, again. She then said, "No."

"No," Marcus repeated.

"Well..." Vasigari said. She glared icily at Marcus. "Perhaps I should just take it."

"You won't."

"I won't...?"

"I can prove you don't exist."

Vasigari stepped back. For the first time since he left Ebon, the truth clicked. He had not the faintest idea how to prove Vasigari did not exist. Indeed, he had not the faintest idea how to prove *anything* did not exist. What he *did* know was that he had the idol. The idol was his only true claim to fame.

He waited for Vasigari to respond. She stood quiet, silent, for what seemed like forever. She then stomped her foot on the ground. Marcus jumped back. "Fine," she said. She tossed another glare Marcus's way.

"Fine..." Marcus said.

Vasigari paused, took a deep breath and said, "You're making an error."

Marcus said, "I'm -"

"A *grave* error," Vasigari interrupted. She pointed her finger at him. "You will regret it."

Before Marcus could respond, she disappeared into everywhere. Marcus pulled the idol out and stared at the figure. He admired its glitter in the sunlight.

- 46 -

Cisero stopped by the inn. Marcus immediately inquired how he knew the idol had been recovered.

"Word travels fast," Cisero said. He smiled. "I have a *proposition.*"

Marcus shifted uncomfortably. He wasn't aware anyone had known. Other than Vasigari, who was angry, and Aspen and Utica, who didn't believe it, nobody else knew.

"Another one?" Marcus asked.

Cisero smiled and nodded. "I have a collection of rare figurines. That idol would look lovely on my mantle."

"Indeed," Marcus said. "But -"

"But?" Cisero asked. "You sound hesitant! Your day has arrived! Why don't we trade? In exchange for the idol, I'll be your personal agent as well as your guide through the conference."

Marcus's eyes grew wide. "Oh!"

"Your personal chauffeur on the road to fame," Cisero said.

Before Marcus could think it through, he exclaimed, "Deal!"

"Excellent," Cisero said. He quickly shook Marcus's hand.

Marcus said quietly, "But I still need the idol."

Vasigari was out of the picture. But he had still promised the idol to two recipients. And, try as he did, he was unable to make two idols exist.

"You still need the idol," Cisero said.

Marcus nodded. "For the proof."

Cisero smirked. "We had a deal."

"I know, I know," Marcus said. "It's just - I meant... *after* the conference."

Cisero held his finger up. He stared out the window for a moment. Marcus smiled hopefully.

"Okay," Cisero said. He grinned. "Hold on to it... *for now*. In fact, things may work out better this way." He pat Marcus on the back.

Marcus smiled. "Oh, thank you!" he exclaimed.

Marcus wondered what would happen after he returned, after he'd given the idol to Peoria's master. He wondered if he could somehow convince Cisero the master stole it. He was surly enough to do such a thing. Marcus laughed to himself.

As Marcus was thinking, Cisero eyed him curiously. "Well, I must finish the preparations. Tomorrow, we shall leave for Rome!" he said

Marcus nodded. He was still not sure what to say at the Coliseum. Vasigari claimed the idol implied the world did not exist. Perhaps he could figure out how it implied exactly the opposite.

29. All Good Questions

"Listen..." Utica said. Marcus's eyes shot up. He had been staring out the window and pondering his upcoming defense. "It's..."

Marcus turned to face Utica and Aspen. Utica hung her head slightly. "It's not your fault."

"Elm?" Marcus asked.

"We don't blame you," Aspen said. "But to be honest, we were mad at you."

"*Were*," Utica said.

Marcus wasn't sure how to respond. He said, "I see."

"But the idol..." Aspen said.

Marcus pulled out the figurine. Aspen nodded at it. "If you say we went to a non-existent island... then, well, we'll believe you."

Marcus nodded.

"I mean... how can we not?" Utica asked. "It's there!"

"Can I see it?" Aspen asked.

Marcus handed over the idol. Aspen tossed it lightly in his hand and inspected it from all angles. He asked, "Are you sure this doesn't exist?"

"It exists now," Marcus said. He pondered a moment. "Or something. I didn't give it to Vasigari."

"You didn't!" Utica exclaimed. "Was she mad?"

"A *little*," Marcus said. Utica snickered. "But... I need to present my research." He straightened his posture and smiled. "Say... in honor of Elm."

Utica smiled. Aspen nodded.

"You'll be famous!" Utica exclaimed.

"Not so fast, though," Marcus said. He sighed and stared at the idol some more. "First, my research must withstand... the peer review. That's what Cisero explained."

"And he would know?" Aspen asked.

Marcus nodded. "Of course. He's the Games Administrator of Rome. He's taking me to the *Conference* at the Coliseum."

"And you're nervous," Utica said.

"If anyone can do it, you can!" Aspen exclaimed.

"Yes," Utica said. "The great Marcus will triumph! We will support you."

Utica and Aspen held hands. Marcus nodded. "It'll be our day! In honor of Elm!"

Utica and Aspen nodded approvingly. "Elm!" they exclaimed.

- 48 -

Marcus paced slowly outside the inn. He held the idol in his hand, inspecting it carefully. He stared and stared at it. No existence proof was granted.

Marcus thought for several moments. "What is a quest for wisdom?"

"It depends on what wisdom is," the highway replied.

Marcus nodded. "I've been pondering what to say tomorrow. Truth be told, I'm worried that the idol itself is nothing. What great speech am I to make in the Coliseum about it?

For I think I gained more wisdom *questing* for the silly thing than I did *from* it."

"Ah!" the highway exclaimed. It chuckled. "Perhaps you see now!"

"That wisdom is a journey?"

"And never-ending at that," the highway replied.

Marcus smiled. He pondered the peculiar object he held in his hand. "Then what of this idol? What does it represent? What do I share with the public?"

"Share what you know!" the highway exclaimed. "They will listen."

"The world is a mysterious place."

"That it is," the highway agreed.

"It is a very *complex* place!" Marcus added.

The highway sat silent for a moment. It asked, "Is that the beauty or the curse?"

Marcus thought about the answer for a moment. "I would argue it is the beauty," he said. "For if it were simple, the opportunities for great journeys would certainly be in short supply!"

"Yes, yes, you have come far," the highway said. "But you have a long way to go, still."

"I still do not know what my original quest was."

The highway grinned. "You will figure it out. I have confidence that you can do it."

"Where does the wind originate from?" Marcus asked. "Where do the water's ripples come from?"

"All questions you should answer."

"I wrote of the world," Marcus said. "I wrote of the curiosities I happened by in nature." He thought of those that he had. He thought of the sway of the pattern of clouds. He thought of standing with Peoria, watching the spiraling leaves. "I wish I had pursued them further," he said. "I think if I had, I might have stumbled upon something big. Something great."

"You have through your writing. You recorded your thoughts. Your ideas," the highway said.

"I suppose all it takes is for someone to come along and suggest there is some mystery waiting to be uncovered," Marcus said. "Something hidden. Something there."

Marcus gazed down the highway. The sun continued to rise. By now, the sky was bright, and the dew drying. "It is a long road," he said.

"It is," the highway agreed. "You are on the verge of a great idea. A great light. And now you know how to go about finding it. Now that you've built a foundation in wisdom, you know the answer. And, the world will certainly never be the same."

30. So Far From Home

I contemplated the road. If this highway really were a path in thought, it didn't seem to promise very much to me. I tried to remember what Warren had said. Something like, "the decisions we make are like the paths in the forest, taking us to different places." On this highway, there was only one direction to go. Up the mountain.

Sheridan seemed *really* good at predicting what I was thinking. If one has no branches on their road, of course it would be easy to predict what they'd do. They'd just be a passenger, watching their own life like a movie. I glanced at Sheridan. For the first time, and not the last, I wondered which one of us was the driver, and which the passenger.

I shook my head clear. Sheridan was watching me. He didn't seem worried at all that I had spaced out while steering the car. He just stared at me with that stupid grin, and continued his story.

- 49 -

Marcus stumbled through the dark. There was no moon, and very few stars were visible under the moving clouds. He had grown accustomed to visiting Peoria in the deep night. They usually met in the fields, but today she met him on the roadway, startling him.

"Peoria!" Marcus exclaimed. "You are so far from home tonight."

Peoria nodded silently. She flashed a brief smile, but quickly returned to her original distraught face. Marcus stroked her cheek. "What's wrong?"

Peoria closed her eyes and shook her head. "I have a bad feeling."

Marcus tilted his head. "A bad feeling?"

Peoria nodded.

"What are you so worried about?" Marcus asked. "Vasigari?"

"I don't know," Peoria said. "She left so..." Marcus lifted an eyebrow. "...abruptly."

"Well... I wouldn't worry about *her*."

Peoria glanced back toward the fields. For several moments they stood in silence.

Marcus stared into the sky. The stars seemed dimmer than usual. He couldn't think why. It bothered him. Peoria watched him. She whispered, "I'll miss you..."

"Why?!" Marcus asked.

"You know I can't leave the fields for too long," Peoria replied.

Marcus stared at her. She repeated, "I have an uneasy feeling about tomorrow... about you going."

"Oh Peoria," Marcus said. He took her hand, "I will find you again... I would track you down to the end of the world."

Peoria quietly nodded. Marcus asked, "So, are we in agreement on the terms, then?"

Peoria closed her eyes and sighed as she struggled to respond with words. Instead, she just smiled. Marcus, too, struggled to say something else. But instead, he just contributed another smile to the awkward silence. Finally, they both said, in unison, "Well... look at the time... I better get some sleep..."

"Good night," Peoria whispered.

"Good night..." Marcus whispered back.

"Close your eyes, sweet dreamer," Peoria sang quietly, smiling.

"Eyes... dreamer... close your sweet," Marcus whispered. He grinned.

As they parted ways, Marcus turned around to steal one last glance at Peoria.

As he disappeared down the path, Peoria slowly stepped aside. She stopped just outside the fields and stared at the stars. She hid her face in her hands and cried. Angry and frustrated with herself, she ran off into the night.

31. Let Us Witness His Feats

For the next half-mile or so, Sheridan and I sat in silence. Sheridan fiddled with the right air vent, watching how the particles of dust swirled in the current. I watched the sky. Again. Sheridan's tales had a way of drawing it to my attention.

I noticed Sheridan was staring. He tilted his head curiously. "Nothing," I said. He tilted his head the other way. "Peoria's tale is depressing," I said.

Sheridan continued to stare. "Nevermind," I said.

"You seem a little distraught about it," he said.

"Nevermind."

Sheridan nodded. We sat in awkward silence for a moment. He tapped on the dash panel. "Nice car."

"I bought it this week. My old one was stolen at the NCSU-UNC tailgate party."

Sheridan snickered. "Oh! I was at that!"

I was surprised to hear Sheridan was there. But stranger things have happened. I *did* pick him up around that area. It wasn't *that* much of a coincidence. I wondered what he was doing there. I asked him.

"Research," he said. He smiled, and started to unfold a piece of paper he took from his pocket.

I glanced at the writing. Unintelligible scribbling, and a date: "12 March."

"What's that?" I asked.

"That," Sheridan said, "is the date the world will end."

Once again, I was reminded I had picked up a nut. I glanced at the sky. *He* was the reason it had started to worry me in the first place.

"Will you stop telling me the world is ending!" I demanded.

Sheridan put the paper back in his pocket. "You did ask, you know."

My curiosity almost got the better of me. I almost asked him how he knew the world was ending. I glanced at the clock. It was a little past midnight, on the eleventh.

But then I started to wonder... what was the rest of his writing? I wished I had gotten a better look at it. I had forgotten the entire point of Sheridan's story - how he ended up on the side of the road. I wondered what the Giant Dachy had to do with it all. I was becoming more and more convinced he wasn't a bum. But that little piece of paper seemed to be the *only* thing he carried. He had no change of clothes, toiletries, or any other luggage that would suggest he was traveling. I would be surprised if he even had a wallet.

I peeked at his pocket. A corner of the paper stuck out. My curiosity of its contents was interrupted by another observation. There was a peculiar bulge that could only be made by one thing - car keys.

- 50 -

The next morning bore a clear, blue sky. A cool breeze rushed in from the North, hoisting the flags of the Coliseum up amongst the clouds. The crowd was anxious and cheering, gearing up for a day of exciting games. They had been promised "a glimpse at a true wonder of the world."

Marcus strolled into the preparation gallery. "Cisero!" he exclaimed.

Cisero replied, "Are you ready?"

"I am!" Marcus said. He patted the bulge in his satchel where the idol sat.

Cisero re-explained the procedure. "Our hosts will announce your presence and then you hold up the idol on their cue. Understand?"

Marcus nodded. "It really is quite simple," Cisero said. He smiled. "They'll ask if you wish to say anything about it. You will have to speak very loudly, and keep your words to a minimum. After the review, I'm sure many people will want to meet you. You can say more then."

"Understood," Marcus said, smiling. "This is truly a grand opportunity."

Cisero grinned. "Indeed. Indeed." He put his arm around Marcus, patted the satchel, and stretched his other arm toward the air. "The day will be yours, my friend!"

The crowd's cheer grew louder as drums rolled outside the gate. Marcus could not hear the hosts over the roar. When the gate opened, Cisero pushed Marcus toward it. "Go!" he exclaimed. "It's time!"

The Coliseum arena was much bigger than Marcus had anticipated. The massive crowd was a blur - a roaring, cheering blur. He told himself not to feel nervous, and looked for where Utica and Aspen might be seated. He was too far from any of the walls to see faces clearly. He began to feel more nervous. He had never addressed such a large crowd before.

Cisero stood on a balcony hung high over the floor. He faced the crowd and shouted, "Friends! Romans! Countrymen! The time has come for the peer review! Lend your ears to... Marcus! Numus! Tullis!"

That must be the cue to hold up the idol! Marcus thought. He wasn't sure if the crowd had been told exactly what he would show them. He tried to think of the best way to explain what the idol was. He reached inside his satchel and pulled out...

nothing!

Marcus froze, stunned. He tried again. Nothing. In a panic, he frantically looked around. *Perhaps I dropped it*, he thought. He looked around again.

"The great warrior of the Giant Dachy returns!" Cisero cried. "Let us witness his feats!"

One word suddenly popped into Marcus's mind. *Vasigari!* He looked around the arena for her. *She stole it!* he thought. *But how?*

Marcus scanned the arena once more. His attention was seized when he noticed several gates along the walls swing open. He tilted his head, curious, just as an angry lion charged out. He remembered Master Sophus's stories of his own experiences at the conference. *The Referee is a ferocious lion... with teeth sharp as knives and the devil's eyes.*

As Marcus watched the great beast burst through the gate, he also felt a twinge of panic - it could very well be that he was too delicious to be a Mathematician, and the Referee wanted nothing more than to gobble him up.

The crowd cheered as more lions drew close on all sides. Marcus looked to the left. Lions. He looked to the right. Lions. *Did Vasigari open the lions' gates?!* he thought. *What is going on?!*

"Show yourself!" he exclaimed. "I know you're everywhere!"

Fully panicked, he ran for the largest lion-less gap. The great beasts ran faster. The crowd cheered Marcus on, anxiously awaiting his proof that the lions didn't exist.

Marcus looked up at the walls. Aspen and Utica sat in the front row, watching in horror. "Utica! Aspen!" he exclaimed.

Utica and Aspen looked at each other.

"We have to help him!" Utica exclaimed. "I don't think he can prove the lions don't exist! There are too many of us watching to confirm that they do!"

"Where's the idol?!" Aspen shouted back.

Utica and Aspen quickly snatched the spears from the guards caught up in the spectacle. By the time they noticed their weapons had been snatched, Utica and Aspen were already at the ledge.

"It's a long way!" Aspen yelled. He turned around. The two guards were closing in on them. "Jump!" he shouted. "To the non!"

Utica grasped her spear firmly against her chest. "To non-existence!"

Marcus cried, "Utica! Aspen! Help!"

Utica hit the ground first, followed by Aspen. Aspen struggled to climb to his feet and find his weapon. Utica groaned as she tried to stand up as well. Failing, she sat back down. "Aspen?" she whispered.

"Yes?" Aspen whispered back, making another attempt to stand.

"This might have been a mistake," Utica replied.

They both looked up and realized just how far they had fallen. Unable to move, they turned their attention back to the jaws of a massive lion.

Marcus tried to find Utica and Aspen amongst the lions. He scanned the arena and noticed a faint sparkle in the sand. *The idol!* he thought. He began to run toward it.

Another lion jumped into his path. Marcus ran around it. The lion swiped its claws at his legs. He tripped and fell face-first into the sand.

He shook off the pain and drove his hand into the ground. His vision was blurred by dirt, but he could make out the sparkle. He reached further and pulled out a tiny, shiny pebble.

Marcus faced forward. The shadow of a lion obstructed his view of the arena. For a few seconds, its teeth remained in his view. Then there was no view at all.

32. The Best Teacher of Wisdom

I looked Sheridan's way and smirked. "What kind of ending was that?"

Sheridan smiled innocently. "What kind of ending was what?"

"*That*," I said. "You can't have spent the past couple hundred miles telling me a story that ends with the hero being *eaten* by a lion!"

"I can't?" Sheridan asked.

I watched the road drift by before replying, "No."

"But that's the way it happened," Sheridan said. "You, of all people, should know that history is the way it is."

I shook my head. "History is the way it is *told*."

Sheridan thought carefully for a moment. "Perhaps... but that doesn't mean what is told really *was*."

"But, you, yourself, said that reality is as we define it."

Lightning arched across the sky. For the first time in a while, I could see the landscape around me. I knew we were high in the mountains. I could barely make out the farmlands below, but at least I saw they were there. We hadn't been sucked up into some abyss. It brought some relief.

"Well, you're right. Reality can be as you define it. But that doesn't mean you can just make up *anything*. It has to fit into the world you interact with. Sometimes things happen that can't be controlled."

I laughed to myself. "You can't propose that *you* have a

'sensible' reality. You have a world in which the highway has words to speak and the brook a phobia of its own fish!"

Sheridan shook his head. "It's not a *phobia*. It's an insecurity. And, perhaps, you just don't know how to listen."

A second cloud-tentacle flashed in front of the windshield. I slammed on the brakes. Sheridan let out a laugh; I let out a scream. The car began to swing wildly across the wet road. One of my textbooks flew off the seat and slammed into the side window. A long, spider-like crack extended from the center of the impact. We spun for a moment, then came to rest on the shoulder.

Thunder roared from afar, its echo bouncing across the mountaintops. Sheridan and I sat in silence. We rested against the guardrail - facing the wrong way down the road. I slowly looked out the side. I could only see a fog-filled abyss. I looked at Sheridan, then gave my analysis of the situation. "Holy shit!"

Sheridan laughed. "It's okay, man. Let it out."

I tossed Sheridan an icy glare. "How can you be so...!" I threw my arms in the air. "What the *hell* is going on!"

Sheridan continued to stare. I took a deep breath. "Okay."

I slowly put the car back into gear and pointed us in the correct direction. I looked ahead. The road seemed to climb higher and higher. Several moments passed before I realized I was only driving 20 or 25 and my hands were shaking. Sheridan didn't say anything. I wondered if he thought *I* was a looney.

Ahead, the road ascended into the clouds and disappeared. We continued to drive up. We could only continue so much further before the clouds would be touching us. I'm wasn't a religious man, but I prayed the road would descend before we hit that ceiling.

- 51 -

Peoria clung to the entry-way gate, stunned by what she saw. Cisero stood in the center of the arena, holding the idol high above his head to the cheers of the crowd.

"Behold! The Idol of Trey!" Cisero shouted. "What I hold here is the result of a great conquest. No doubt you have heard the legends. Now, here is the proof! The wisdom of hundreds of years in a matter of seconds."

"Traitor!" Peoria whispered as she watched Cisero parade the idol around the arena.

Cisero continued, "No doubt I am now wise! And you who are present shall reap wisdom as well! Gaze into the idol! Behold what wisdom reaps! Behold me! For now I am all-knowing!"

The roar of a stray, forgotten lion interrupted Cisero's speech. The cheering of the crowd abruptly stopped as Cisero slowly turned around to face eye-to-teeth with the monstrous beast.

"Hi..." Cisero said quietly as he let the idol hit the ground. The crowd gasped in horror as both Cisero and the Idol of Trey were quickly devoured.

- 52 -

You promised you would find me again she thought. *How are you going to do that now?*

Peoria looked up at evening the sky and shouted, "How are you going to do that now?"

"You promised you would set me free!" she exclaimed. "To snatch me away! How will you do that now?"

She closed her eyes and shook her head. She quietly repeated, "How will you do that now?"

She looked down, toward the highway. The road curved and carved its way through the forest. She thought of what Marcus had said of the highway. She thought of his unfinished quest. She remembered he'd kept a roll of paper on which he recorded his thoughts and discoveries. She suddenly realized he may not have brought it to the conference.

Peoria frantically ran back to the inn. She rummaged through his desk, looking for the roll of paper. If she could preserve his work, it might bring her some relief. She pulled an empty spindle out of the drawer. She held the tube to her heart, then collapsed to the floor, crying.

- 53 -

Peoria felt a tap on her shoulder. She looked up at the strange woman - tall, with long, straight black hair and maroon clothing. The woman smiled reassuringly. Peoria recognized her from Marcus's writings. "You're the one that sent Marcus away."

Vasigari lifted an eyebrow. "Away?"

"To SanCullep Island," Peoria said. She sneered. "To find that ridiculous idol."

"Yes," Vasigari said. "But I fear I was not aware of the nature of the *monster*. For now that SanCullep exists, the *monster* does, too. Marcus never did prove the island back *out* of existence. And it seems our friend Cisero was a friend of the Temple of the Night Song."

Vasigari looked out the window and sighed. "Cisero didn't want Marcus to prove the world existed. He wanted to know how to write such a proof so he could prove SanCullep and the cult existed. That's why he wanted the idol. Who knows what he did with it before he marched out into that arena."

Peoria continued to stare blankly. Vasigari smiled cheerfully as she headed toward the door. "I think Marcus will prove to be a great hero."

Peoria choked back tears and asked, "How?" She glared at Vasigari. "In case you didn't notice..."

"Oh, I noticed," Vasigari said. She turned around and looked Peoria straight in the eye. "But we had a deal. And I won't let something as trivial as *death* leave my promise unfulfilled."

Vasigari started to walk away. She stopped abruptly, pulled out Marcus's roll of paper, and tossed it to Peoria. As Vasigari disappeared into everywhere, Peoria stared at the roll.

33. Pseudo-Random Arches

With the sky hovering so close, I'd begun to lose focus on Sheridan's tale. Each time I calmed down enough to drive faster, another tentacle would shoot down. Sheridan didn't seem to mind, but it was all I could do to keep my eyes focused on the road.

I laughed at myself. Why was I so jumpy? They were just clouds, after all. I'd flown before, and I remembered the airplane just went right through them. Fog was just low cloud-cover... harmless.

We passed a tentacle that shot down onto a tree. I forced myself to laugh at it. I glanced in my rearview mirror. The tentacle was gone. The smile dropped from my face. So was the tree.

"You look pale, John," Sheridan said.

"The clouds!" I exclaimed. "It..." I glanced in the rear mirror again. "The clouds!"

Sheridan stared at me. I exclaimed, "Why do you keep staring at me?"

Sheridan scratched his head. "You seem a little tense."

"Well, hell, Sheridan," I said. "You tell me the world is ending! And no sooner than we almost wreck... twice! *What* is happening with the sky?"

We were crawling... maybe only 15 miles per hour. The road continued to ascend.

As we rounded a corner, I caught a good look at the

mountaintops. I distinctly remembered them being in view before. Now, the peaks were obscured.

I slammed on the gas. Sheridan flew back into his seat and made a face that looked like a scream; I'm pretty sure he was saying "Wheeee!" though. I couldn't hear him over the engine. He looked at me like I had gone mad, and perhaps I had. But it clicked - if the clouds were descending, we had to get over the pass.

The logical side of me said I was being foolish. But the part of me that didn't want to be eaten by a demon-cloud told me to *drive*.

"A little worried?" Sheridan asked. For the first time, he wasn't smiling.

The wind began to howl - ferociously. Trees swayed violently and rain began to splatter the windshield. "You're damn right!" I exclaimed.

And then, Sheridan took my hand. He began to hum. I glanced his way. He said, "Mingo and I once took a flight together... she's afraid of the turbulence. I told her it was the wind-dragons playing with the airplane. But they wouldn't do it any harm."

I stole another glance. He was staring into the sky, just as calm as could be. He said, "They were just guiding the plane. That's their job."

I swerved around a fallen branch. We skidded slightly off the road. A huge wave shot up from behind the car. We righted ourselves and I slammed on the gas again. Sheridan continued to hum. "The world won't end without us!"

"Will you *stop* telling me the world is ending?" I exclaimed. "You're freaking me out!"

"But it is," Sheridan said. "And I'm telling you why. I owe you an explanation."

"Oh, you owe me more than that," I said.

The sky loomed just above our heads. Tentacles swooped

down all across the road. I slowed just enough to swerve around them. Sheridan continued to stare silently. With a large *thud*, we hit a fallen tree branch. Splinters showered up the back of the car and disappeared into the wind.

And then, we reached the top. We began descending. The sky began to grow distant. Sheridan arched his neck to look up at it.

Another moment later, the wind died. The rain stopped. The road was calm. I pulled over for a moment to catch my breath.

We sat in silence. Tentacles still descended from the sky, but we were far out of their reach. I looked Sheridan's way. He nodded. "It's a long road," he said.

"Tell me about it."

Sheridan chuckled. I shook my head.

I stole another glance at the sky. "Tell me... that explanation."

Sheridan smiled. "I'd be happy to."

I focused on the highway. "Please look after us," I whispered under my breath.

The highway did not respond.

I caught a red flash out the rear window. It was a leaf reflecting the brake lights. It floated in the car's wake, dancing in wild, random arches. In fact, they might have even been pseudo-random.

Wouldn't it be amazing to open the world and see what was inside? To dance in its rays and hold it in your palm? Wouldn't it be wonderful... to be a part of it all?

As the clouds continue their descent, John begins to wonder if Sheridan isn't just an ordinary hitchhiker. He wonders about the patterns Marcus described, and why he is noticing them as well. Perhaps the solution lies with the discoveries of Mara, a young girl living in the Renaissance. What she unravels reveals to John a truth about Sheridan, the highway, and himself, with far graver implications than he would ever care to contemplate.

Sheridan's saga continues with the second stage:

AN EMBER IN THE WIND

Keep up to date by visiting the blog at:

http://www.anorthogonaluniverse.com

For news on the sequel, visit:

http://www.anemberinthewind.com

Like this book? Scan and share with your mobile device!

Thanks for reading!

Robert L. Watson wrote the first draft of *A Foundation in Wisdom* ~~instead of~~ while studying for the qualifying exam in Linear and Lie Algebra at North Carolina State University. He is now a Mathematics professor at Mount Olive College, where he still appreciates mathematical fantasies (the most creative of which involve late assignments). He lives in Mount Olive with his wife, Elizabeth, and cats Milton and Spenser.

Acknowledgements

The production of this book has been helped along by many people over the years. My deepest gratitude is reserved for my wife, Elizabeth Watson, to whom the story was originally written for, and whose support has encouraged me to share it with the world. Also particularly deserving of my thanks are Hazel, Tom, and Melissa Watson, for their encouragement.

Much of the story was inspired by late night conversations with the residents of the University of Tulsa Honors House, a frequent occurence during my undergraduate days.

A special thanks goes to Kisa Whipkey of Nightwolf Art & Design, whose editorial guidance helped shape the original manuscript into the book you're holding.